The BIG SHOWDOWN

MICKEY SPILLANE
AND
MAX ALLAN COLLINS

The BIG SHOWDOWN

A CALEB YORK WESTERN

KENSINGTON BOOKS
http://www.kensingtonbooks.com

KENSINGTON BOOKS are published by

Kensington Publishing Corp.
119 West 40th Street
New York, NY 10018

All Kensington titles, imprints, and distributed lines are available at special quantity discounts for bulk purchases for sales promotion, premiums, fund-raising, educational, or institutional use.

Special book excerpts or customized printings can also be created to fit specific needs. For details, write or phone the office of the Kensington Special Sales Manager: Attn. Special Sales Department. Kensington Publishing Corp, 119 West 40th Street, New York, NY 10018. Phone: 1-800-221-2647.

Kensington and the K logo Reg. U.S. Pat. & TM Off.

Library of Congress Card Catalogue Number: 2015958940

ISBN-13: 978-1-61773-596-7
ISBN-10: 1-61773-596-5
First Kensington Hardcover Edition: May 2016

eISBN-13: 978-1-61773-597-4
eISBN-10: 1-61773-597-3
First Kensington Electronic Edition: May 2016

10 9 8 7 6 5 4 3 2 1

Printed in the United States of America

For my old pard,
Ed Gorman,
master of the noir Western

"All the screen cowboys (before me) behaved like real gentlemen. They didn't drink, they didn't smoke. When they knocked the bad guy down, they always stood with their fists up, waiting for the heavy to get back on his feet. I decided I was going to drag the bad guy to his feet and keep hitting him."

—John Wayne

CALEB YORK, JOHN WAYNE, AND MICKEY SPILLANE

In the mid- to late 1950s, Mickey Spillane took a break from writing novels about his famous detective character, Mike Hammer, and tried any number of other things.

Some of this was man's-man-style wish-fulfillment—racing stock cars, deep-sea diving, getting shot out of a cannon (with the Clyde Beatty Circus, where he was also a trampoline artist). Other endeavors were an extension of his position as the most popular fiction writer of his time—writing a Hammer comic strip, recording a Hammer record album, and appearing on TV (spoofing himself on *The Milton Berle Show*, for example).

Spillane was also heavily involved with various film and TV projects, including writing a live-action episode of the *Suspense* TV show, developing projects for Berle and another famous Mickey (Rooney), and writing non-Hammer screenplays in several genres. He even developed an anthology series with *Star Trek* creator, Gene Roddenberry, wherein he would be the Hitchcock-style host; but the *Mike Hammer* series TV producers complained and the show never came to fruition.

In addition, Mickey wrote and directed his own short Hammer film (apparently lost), showcasing his choice for the role by way of his New Jersey cop friend, Jack Stang, a decorated Marine veteran of World War II. Appearing with Stang were legendary comedian Jonathan Winters and Bettye Ackerman, later the female lead on TV's *Ben Casey*.

The Hammer "test film" project—written up in several magazines of the day—reflected Mickey's dissatisfaction with what producer Victor Saville was doing with the Spillane properties the esteemed British director/producer was bringing to the screen. While appreciation for the 1953 3-D film version of *I, the Jury* has grown among film *noir* afficionados, and Robert Aldrich's 1955 adaptation of *Kiss Me, Deadly* is now considered a classic, Spillane at the time was frustrated at being frozen out of the film-making process by Saville. Mickey wanted a hand in the writing and the casting, while Saville made promises that were never kept, just "handling" the famous blue-collar writer.

Actor John Wayne and his producing partner, Robert Fellows, were friends of Mickey's, and decided to give the frustrated Mike Hammer creator a chance to show what he and Jack Stang could do, by casting them in the circus picture *Ring of Fear* (1954). Mickey played himself, a famous mystery writer, and Stang played an implied Hammer. Two things backfired, but in a good way.

First, Mickey blew Stang off the screen. The tough but affable Mickey, a natural before the camera, was clearly the Mike Hammer character come to life, while Stang remained in the background, big, looming, but making little impact. Second, producer Wayne was unhappy with the footage being shot and asked Mickey to rewrite the picture into more of a suspense movie and not just a backstage-at-the-circus piece. Director William Wellman was brought in to shoot the new Spillane-scripted footage. On an earlier occasion, Mickey and Wayne were at a rough-cut screening of another Wellman picture, and the famed director was having problems with a key scene.

Wayne said, "Mickey knows what's wrong with it. Tell him, Mickey."

And Spillane told "Wild Bill" Wellman how to restructure the footage, giving the great director editing advice that was gratefully embraced.

As for *Ring of Fear* (available on DVD), Mickey declined any screen credit for his rewrite, or for that matter payment. So producer Wayne had a white Jaguar convertible, which he'd seen Mickey admiring in a Los Angeles showroom, delivered to the writer's home in Newburgh, New York, the little sports car wrapped in a red ribbon, with a card signed, "Thanks—Duke."

The John Wayne/Mickey Spillane friendship included the writer being invited to occasional screenings for his input, whenever the mystery writer happened to be out in Hollywood. But it also extended, on one memorable occasion, to Mickey's services as a screenwriter.

The existing correspondence in Mickey's files from Wayne doesn't make it clear which man initiated the Western project. At the very least Wayne expressed his enthusiasm for a Spillane-written Western. Mickey told me that *The Saga of Cali York* (as it was originally titled) was intended for Wayne himself, and had been commissioned by the actor; but it's also possible that Wayne might have handed *York* off to Randolph Scott, Glenn Ford, or Robert Mitchum, who starred in various Wayne-produced films of the era, or some other appropriate star.

About the time Mickey would have turned in his screenplay, Wayne's production company was suffering financial woes due to the out-of-control budget—exacerbated by later box-office disappointment—of *The Alamo* (1960).

While Wayne's company Batjac eventually recovered, the superstar for a time had to make pictures for other producers and various studios, to dig himself out of the hole his pet project had dug.

Wayne's now ex-producing partner, Bob Fellows, went on to team up with Mickey on two films, *The Girl Hunters* (1963) and *The Delta Factor* (1970), both from Spillane novels. The latter film is minor, but *The Girl Hunters* (now on DVD and Blu-ray) is significant if for no other reason than Spillane himself played Mike Hammer and co-wrote the screenplay. The persona Mickey presented in *The Girl Hunters* became the basis of the self-spoofing one he used when appearing in the enormously successful Miller Lite commercials of the 1980s and '90s (with "doll" Lee Meredith of *The Producers* fame).

Over the years, I heard Mickey speak fondly of Wayne, and the Wayne screenplay, any number of times, and while not a man given to expressing regrets, Mickey clearly wished the *York* project had come to light. The writer often said that Mike Hammer was a modern-day Western hero ("He wore the black hat but he did the right thing") and Spillane felt a kinship with the Western genre.

Shortly before his death in 2006, Mickey indicated to his wife, Jane, that I should be given his files, and asked to complete various unfinished projects—an amazing honor. This included at least nine Mike Hammer novels in various stages of development, several other unfinished crime novels, and a handful of movie scripts. Of the latter, *York* jumped out at me.

The Legend of Caleb York, published in 2015 by Kensington Books, is essentially a novelization of Mickey's unproduced screenplay. My editor, Michaela Hamilton—

long a Spillane fan—has asked me to continue the saga of Caleb York, drawing upon various drafts of the screenplay and notes in Mickey's files.

Mickey provided York with a rich back story as a Wells Fargo agent, which I may yet explore; but my wife, Barb (my collaborator on the "Trash 'n' Treasures" mysteries), suggested I write a direct sequel that further explores the characters, conflicts, and world Mickey created in his screenplay.

The Big Showdown is that sequel.

Again, picturing John Wayne as Caleb York is permitted but not required. I lean a little to Randolph Scott myself. Barb pictures Joel McCrea. And I bet Mickey wasn't picturing Wayne, either.

He was likely seeing, in his mind's eye, a guy named Spillane.

—Max Allan Collins

CHAPTER ONE

Caleb York was getting out of town on the noon stage. Despite his reputation as a deadly gunfighter, York was not being run out of Trinidad, New Mexico, by the sheriff. After all, until very recently, York had been the sheriff here himself, a position he'd held down for six months until a replacement could be found for the previous holder of that office.

It was the least York could do for the dusty little community, considering he'd killed the man.

Not that Sheriff Harry Gauge hadn't needed killing—a petty tyrant seeking to become a cattle baron, a ruthless murderer that the West was well rid of. But removing Gauge from the Trinidad scene, on the heels of a cowpox epidemic, had left the town in something of a topsy-turvy mess. The Trinidad Citizens Committee had asked York to pick up Gauge's badge, wipe the filth from it, and pin it on. At least for a while.

This York had done.

But now he'd found a suitable replacement in his old friend Ben Wade, who'd been a lawman in Kansas and Arizona, working alongside the likes of the Earp brothers and Bat Masterson. Even at fifty-some, Wade was twice the man of most anyone he was likely to come up against.

Right now York was walking down the boardwalk, its awning shading him from morning sun, mercilessly bright in a clear sky, though the temperature on this dry, lightly breezy September morning was around sixty degrees. He was on his way to the office that had been his till he turned it over to Wade last week.

Townspeople nodded at York, and he nodded back, casting smiles at the men, tipping his hat to the ladies. He was unaware that many of the latter turned to look at him as he passed, with wistful smiles and the occasional girlish giggle. Even from the older ones.

York indeed made a fine figure of a man, long of leg, broad of shoulder, firm of jaw, his hair reddish brown, his face clean-shaven, his features pleasant, rawboned, with washed-out blue eyes that peered out a permanent squint. He had settled easily into that vague space between thirty and forty when a man was at his best and, in the case of a Caleb York, his most dangerous. His Colt Single Action Army .44 rode his right thigh at pocket level, the holster tie loose and dangling; his spurs sang an easygoing, jingling song.

When he'd ridden into town last year, those who didn't know how to look at a man saw only a dude, and York still dressed in a manner unlike either the cowhands of the surrounding ranches that Trinidad served, or the shopkeepers who did the serving. York considered his somewhat citified attire professional, and it reflected the time he'd spent in big cities like Denver and Tucson.

But even Trinidad's few professional men—Doc Miller, the bankers, the lawyers—did not approach the sartorial flair of Caleb York, who wore black as did they, only with touches of style—gray trim on collars and cuffs, gray string tie, twin breast pockets, pearl buttons down his shirt, black cotton pants tucked into hand-tooled black boots, curl-brimmed black hat with cavalry pinch, gray kerchief knotted at the neck.

But ever since Caleb York had gunned down Gauge and half a dozen of his hardcase deputies, no one in Trinidad had called him "dude."

If pressed, he'd have admitted that he would miss this prospering little town of three hundred, and the surrounding ranchers and their families and hands who kept it thriving. Not that there was anything particularly special about the place.

One end of Main Street—the dust kept down by a layer of sand brought in from the nearby Purgatory River—was home to a white wooden church, the other end a bare-wood livery stable, steeple and high-peaked hayloft mirroring each other. Between them was a typical collection of businesses—hardware store, apothecary, barber, hotel with restaurant, telegraph, saloon, café—false-fronted clapboards and now and then a brick building, like the bank.

As he neared the livery stable, York felt a twinge—his black-maned, dappled gray gelding was in a stall within that homely structure. The blacksmith, Clem Wiggins, would sell the steed and wire the proceeds to him in San Diego. It might take a while, because the animal was worth a small fortune—less than five hundred would be horse theft. But even twice that couldn't make up for the loss of a loyal steed like that.

He doubted he'd even need a horse in San Diego. That would likely be a city where you either walked or hopped an electric streetcar. Where the only horses you saw were attached to buggies or milk wagons. A different world, but a world he needed to learn to live in.

He was nearing the scarred, bullet-pocked adobe building that wore a high-up sign saying SHERIFF'S OFFICE AND JAIL. Across the way was a handful of smaller adobes, the homes and businesses of the town's modest Mexican population. He took the few steps up to the wooden porch, sheltered by an awning, and knocked at the rough-wood door, a solid thing that could help make the office a fortress when need be.

"It's open!" a deep voice boomed.

York went in and took off his hat.

The office was a plank-floored space with two barred windows onto the street, a wood-burning stove, and a rough-hewn table overseen by a wall of wanted posters and a rack of rifles. This was at left; at right was a big dark wooden desk with a chair behind it and a man in the chair.

Ben Wade was white-haired and white-mustached and wore his white flat-brim, Canadian-creased hat indoors as well as out, probably to hide where he was balding. Wade was a mite touchy about his age, since most gunfighters didn't live as long as he had. The lawman had a well-fed look that replaced the leanness York had first known in him, when Wade was a deputy marshal in Dodge City.

Wade, in a light blue shirt and tan cowhide vest, was making a cigarette. "Find a chair, Caleb," he said.

York pulled one up and sat down. "Nice to see a geezer like you with such a steady hand."

The sheriff licked the paper, finished making the smoke, and fired it up with a kitchen match. Waved it out. "You're not that young yourself, friend."

"No. I'm not. That's why I'm headed to the big town."

Wade shuddered. "Exactly where I don't want to be. Six years in Denver, working as a hotel house dick. You don't want to know the horrors I seen."

"Pay was good."

"Costs plenty living in a big town. You'll see. But your loss is my gain."

York gestured toward a window. "It's a decent little town, Ben. Your biggest worry is the handful of Gauge's men who're still out there. Gunnies pretendin' they're ranch hands."

He nodded. "You told me such enough times that I'm startin' to pay attention. But ex-gunnies have to make an honest living, too. Times have changed. Times are changing."

"Not that much, Ben, not in Trinidad. Maybe over in Las Vegas, since the train come in. But this little town—could be twenty years ago, and you'd never know it."

"Cowboys still get drunk on payday," Ben said, with a deep chuckle and nod of agreement, "and kids who read too many dime novels will always try to play gunfighter. And die young like those who went before them."

"Old gunfighters who hang on too long, they die, too. Don't forget that, Ben."

"Judas Priest, Caleb," the sheriff said, letting out blue smoke, leaning forward. "*You* got in touch with *me*. You got sudden second thoughts about leavin' this little slice of heaven? You tryin' to talk me out of this job? You want this badge, son, you'll have to rip it off my shirt. Because I am right where I want to be."

"How does Hazel feel about it?"

He flinched, took another deep draw on the smoke. "She's, uh . . . not happy. She likes her house in Denver.

She likes her creature comforts. Our son and his daughters live there, you know."

"Hell, I didn't mean to bust up your happy home."

Wade shook his head. "She'll get over it. One of these days, the stage'll pull up and she'll step off. Mark my words. She was beautiful once, but now she's old and fat like me. She knows I'm the only man on God's good earth who looks at her with eyes that still see beauty. She'll show."

York twitched half a frown. "I hope you're right. I don't need *that* on my conscience."

Wade's laugh exhaled smoke. "Since when does Caleb York *have* a conscience? How many men you put down, anyways?"

"I don't rightly know."

Wade's mustached grin filled a bunch of his face. "Sure you do, son. Only the crazy ones don't keep track. You're hard, but you ain't crazy. How many?"

". . . Twenty-seven."

"Countin' the war?"

"Not counting the war, Ben. You never really know in war how many you put down."

"How do you sleep at night?"

"Fine."

"Bad dreams?"

"Only if I got a fever."

"Good. So I guess I can risk troubling your damn conscience. I got the job I want—this is how I want to spend my last working years. With a badge and a gun and a desk and a chair . . . and a hundred a month. More than that, with my cut of the taxes I collect."

"Much more. It's a good-paying job. I'm glad you're pleased. I hope Hazel comes around."

Wade was nodding. "She'll come around. She'll step off that stage. You'll see."

"Speaking of stages," York said, and stood. "I have one to catch, in about an hour."

Wade gave York another face-splitting grin. "I have a bottle in this desk, if it ain't too early for you. You can spend the rest of your time in Trinidad tellin' me how sorry you are you got me this job I so dearly wanted."

York grinned back, snugging on his hat. "No, I have an early lunch date."

"Certain pretty gal?"

"Certain pretty gal."

"And I reckon she's not real happy with you, is she, son?"

"No. Not happy at all."

"Well, then that's a knack we share."

"What is?"

"Disappointin' our womenfolk."

York gave his old friend a smile and a nod, then went back out into the pleasant morning. Last night, however, had not been so pleasant. That was when he'd told Willa Cullen that he would be leaving at noon today.

Both Willa and her father had been seated at the big carved Spanish-style dining-room table in the rustic ranch house of the Bar-O. They were having coffee in china cups.

Willa, typically, wore a red-plaid shirt and denims, her straw-yellow hair up and braided in back. Her mother had been Swedish and that came through in pretty features and an hourglass figure. Tall, sturdy of frame, Willa was feminine, but in a Viking kind of way. And right now she looked like she'd be pleased to send him to Valhalla.

Or maybe someplace more southern-ward.

Seated across from York, she met his news with cold eyes and flaming cheeks. At the head of the table sat her father, George Cullen, his white hair thin as desert grass, his eyes milky with blindness.

A big man made smaller by time, Cullen wore a white shirt and a black string tie, his strong, white-mustached face undercut by sunken cheeks, his flesh gray from too much time of late spent indoors. Blind men did not ride the range with their cowhands, no matter how much they might want to.

The old man was first to respond. "I'm disappointed, my boy. I reckoned you and Willa here . . . I'd *hoped* . . ."

York said nothing, looking away from the man's milky gaze.

Cullen stuck out his hand, still rough from work, despite how little of it he'd been able to do these last few years. York shook the man's hand. Across from him, Willa was a pretty stick of dynamite trying not to explode.

"Won't be the same around here," Cullen said. "We've come to think of you as part of the family. Be that as it may, we remain in your debt. Without you, this ranch would be lost to us. That cur Harry Gauge might well be sitting here, where I am . . . and I would be under the ground."

"Hard to say," York said. "Your men were there, backing you. In a pinch, the townspeople came through. But I'm happy to have pitched in."

Willa's hands were clenched into small, trembling fists, held before her on the table like those of a child about to throw a tantrum. The red was fading from her cheeks, but her chin was crinkling and trembling and her eyes were tearing up.

Cullen was smiling, his blank eyes looking past York. "You know, my boy, I thought perhaps I might make a rancher out of you. With no son of my own . . ."

"You have Willa. She can run this ranch. She'd be better at it than most men. Maybe *any* man . . . because you raised her, Mr. Cullen."

Tears were rolling down the young woman's cheeks, but she made no effort to wipe them away, her hands still fists.

"You may be right," Cullen said. "But it's a hard road for a woman to travel alone. I won't be here forever. She'd be better with a man at her side. And perhaps one day she'll find herself one."

Willa got up, her chair scraping on the floor like a wheel coming off a wagon, startling her father, who bounced in his chair some.

Cullen said, *"Girl!"*

But she was already out of the room.

York said, "She's upset with me."

Cullen smiled. "Well, I don't need eyes to see that, son. Let her cool off some. Are you heading to San Diego? To that Pinkerton position you meant to fill, afore you got sidetracked in Trinidad?"

"That's right, sir. I'd be number two man in the office, but I won't be abandoned behind a desk. I'd be leading investigations. I'd be out on manhunts."

"I hope you know I wish you the best of luck. Should you get out there and it don't suit you, come back here to us. You'll always have a place at this table, and in our hearts."

York rose and rested a hand on the old man's shoulder and squeezed. Cullen put his hand on York's and squeezed back.

"Don't you go forgetting us now," the old man said.

"Not hardly."

She was on the porch in the moonlight. The ivory of it

suited her. She'd wiped away the tears now, but her lush full lips were trembling.

"I'm sorry to just spring it on you," York said. "But you knew that I was just taking the sheriff post temporary."

She nodded. Swallowed. She either didn't want to speak to him or couldn't.

He risked a tiny smile. "Would you do a thoughtless lout a small favor?"

She glared at him.

"See me off tomorrow? The stage leaves at noon. Maybe we could have a late breakfast or early lunch—around eleven, there at the hotel?"

She said nothing.

"Would you do that for me, sweetheart?"

She turned toward him, eyes and nostrils flaring like a rearing horse. He might have slapped her, judging by the reaction.

But then she'd done something truly surprising: she nodded, and rushed back inside the ranch house.

When he exited the sheriff's office, York almost bumped into a familiar figure, standing there waiting like an eager puppy dog: that old desert rat Tulley, skinny and white-bearded, but that beard barbered now, and the baggy canvas pants washed in recent memory and under blue suspenders a clean BVD top. The bowlegged town character had dried out, at York's encouragement.

"I seen ya go in there," Tulley said in the good-natured rasp that was what was left of a voice ravaged by years of smoke and drink. "You don't think I'd let ya leave town without an *adios*, do you, Sheriff?"

The unlikely friendship between the two men had grown

out of Tulley befriending the stranger who'd ridden into town and into the middle of nasty doings.

"I'm not the sheriff anymore," York reminded him.

"And a damn shame! Damn shame all around. You had a good thing goin' in this here hamlet, Sheriff. Good pay, respect, folks looked up to ye . . . and then there's that yellow-haired gal. You *know* when ol' Cullen finally up and croaks, that ranch'll be hers. You *do* know what you're walkin' out on, don't you?"

"I know, Tulley."

"And friends like Jonathan R. Tulley don't grow on trees neither, you know."

"I suppose not."

Tulley's face clenched like a fist. "Then to hell with you, Caleb York. I may jus' go back to drinkin', jus' find me a bottle and crawl back in, and whose fault will it be?"

"Mine?"

"*Yours!* Your and yours alone. So to hell with you, you selfish son of a bitch."

Then Tulley gave York a big, startling hug, and almost ran back to the stable. He might have been crying.

York was laughing, gently. Who'd ever have thought that *that* old reprobate would be one of the things he'd miss most about Trinidad?

He walked back to the hotel where he checked out and left his packed carpetbag with Wilson, the weak-chinned, pince-nez-sporting clerk who'd given him a register to sign, all those months ago. The .44 in its holster with cartridge-laden gun belt was tucked in the bag, right on top. No need for a weapon on his hip, riding on a stage or a train, not in these times. Why not be comfortable?

At eleven A.M., the hotel dining room, with its dark wood, fancy chairs, and linen tablecloths, was all but empty. A pair of business types were having a late break-fast of bacon and eggs, and a young lovey-dovey couple just passing through were having an early lunch of oyster stew, a specialty of the Trinidad House Hotel.

Willa was seated by the window, a vision in a mote-floating shaft of soft sunlight, looking not at all the tomboy or cowgirl, but the lovely young woman she was. No plaid shirt or Levi's today—she was in that navy-and-white calico dress that he liked so well on her. Nothing fancy, just a simple, feminine frock. That yellow hair was piled high with little curls decorating her smooth forehead.

Nothing of last night's girl holding back tears and anger could be seen in today's self-composed young woman. She even smiled when she saw him enter the dining room. He left his hat on a hook near the entry and joined her.

"Thank you, Willa," he said.

"For . . . ?"

"For meeting me. For seeing me off. I wasn't sure you'd come."

Her smile was a pursed thing, like a kiss she was about to throw. "Neither was I. But I felt I should apologize for my behavior last night."

"Nothing to apologize about."

She shook her head and all that glorious hair moved a little. "You never lied to me. You made it clear you would be leaving one day. One day soon. I had no right to think otherwise."

"Willa, this frontier life . . . it's going to be over one of these days. And I want something else. I haven't asked you to come with me because I knew you wouldn't."

Her eyebrows rose. "That's a little presumptuous, isn't it?"

"No. I know you're going to stick by your father. As well you should. Long as he's alive, and the Bar-O is chugging along, you need to be at his side. Perhaps some day, after he's gone . . . perhaps you'll decide running a ranch isn't for you."

Her eyebrows were back down, but the eyes themselves were half-lidded. "What else might I do with my life, Caleb?"

"You could join me in San Diego."

"Why—is there another position open with the Pinkertons?"

She was teasing him, but in a way that said, behind her adult attitude, the angry child still lurked.

"There's an opening for you, all right. As my wife."

A tiny laugh. "You're proposing marriage, minutes before boarding the stage out of town?"

He nodded. "I'm not offering you a ring. I'm not asking for a commitment. You are free to live your life."

She flushed a little. "Well, that's very generous of you, Caleb."

He reached across the table and touched her hand. That she did not draw it away from his was a relief.

"Sweetheart," he said, "if your feeling for me cools, if someone comes along who fits better into your life . . . is the right kind of man to run the Bar-O with you . . . I would never stand in your way."

She laughed just a little. Her eyes were sad but not tearing. "You have a peculiar way of telling a girl you love her, Caleb York."

"Well, I do, Willa. But the time has to be right. And the situation has to suit us both. Or we'll just be another one of these unhappy couples, hitched to each other like mules to a buckboard."

"No one sweet-talks like you, Caleb."

He shook his head. "I just can't ask you to wait for me. I won't be coming back to Trinidad."

"Not even to visit?"

"Well . . . maybe then. And maybe you could take a trip to San Diego on occasion. Very beautiful. Lots of ocean. Will you write me, Willa?"

"Will you write me?"

"Sure. With my well-known line of sweet talk."

They were smiling at each other now.

So they ordered lunch, both having the oyster stew— amazing what the cook back there could do with tins of those things—and Willa took tea, York coffee. They chatted, mostly about Willa's plans for the ranch. The buyers had paid well for the herd last spring and things were looking up.

"I'm a bit surprised," she said, "that you're leaving before Zachary Gauge gets to town."

Zachary was Harry Gauge's cousin, from somewhere back East, and word around Trinidad was that he'd inherited the late sheriff's property. Much speculation had been bandied about as to the cousin's intentions, since the sheriff had bought over half-a-dozen spreads in his efforts to secure the area's cattle trade, and had owned half-interests in many of the town businesses.

York said, "I thought it best he and I not meet."

"Because you're the man who killed his cousin? Maybe he'll shake your hand—you're *also* the man who made him rich."

"Not so rich," York said.

The meal was done, dishes cleared, and they were on their respective second cups of tea and coffee.

"But he owns all of those spreads," Willa said. "That Harry Gauge made a powerful big landgrab, after all."

"Yeah, but the new owner will be cattle poor. The

beeves were all destroyed, remember, because of the pox. And the business owners have hired a lawyer from Albuquerque to represent them in getting back control of their shops."

"Could they do that?"

York sipped coffee, nodded. "Our late, unlamented sheriff was running an extortion scheme. The shopkeepers of Trinidad were coerced into partnerships and then bullied into repaying 'loans' for the money Harry Gauge put up. They have a good case."

Willa sipped her tea, shrugged. "Well, any way you look at it, Zachary Gauge is going to own a lot of land. Control more of the range than the Bar-O and the remaining smaller spreads put together."

"Let's hope Zachary is a better man than his cousin."

She sat forward. Nothing but earnestness colored her voice now. "Don't you think you should stay, and find out? Wouldn't it depress you terribly to learn everything you and I and Papa and everyone went through, last year, was for naught?"

He smiled. "Darn good argument, Willa. You'll know where to find me if things get out of hand."

She smiled back. "I'll know where to find you. And you'll know where to find me."

The stage would be rolling in soon. He asked her to walk him out and she did, slipping her arm in his. He grabbed his hat off the hook and put it on. Just outside the hotel, on the boardwalk, with no one around, she took his hands in hers and looked up at him with a heartbreaking smile. There, in the middle of town, they were all alone.

"You do *know*, Caleb, that you could have . . . *been with me,* if you wanted. You know I feel that deeply about you. About this. About us."

He gave her a gentle smile. "Well, we did get a little frisky at times."

She blushed. But she said, "You could have had me, Caleb. You still could. You still *can*."

He touched her smooth cheek. "That can wait for our wedding night."

"It doesn't have to."

"It does. And, anyway—"

The sharp report of a handgun, only slightly muffled, stopped him, from across the street.

First Bank of Trinidad.

He took her in his arms, but not to kiss her, rather to spirit her inside where he said, "Get down. On the floor, now!"

She did. She'd been around gunfire before.

Another muffled gunshot. Yelling.

He flew to the check-in desk and the clerk was gone. Getting back around behind it, he found the little chinless buzzard cowering. But the carpetbag was right there, and York got into it, and yanked the Colt from its holster and ran out.

He hurtled the boardwalk railing and landed solid on the sand, .44 in hand, angled slightly up. Directly across the way, the three-story brick bank building sat imposingly on the corner. Out front at the hitching rail waited three black mustangs, looking calm as a millpond, unruffled by the sound of gunfire.

Not a good sign.

He'd barely landed when the first man blew out of the bank, running for his tethered horse; he wore jeans, a work shirt, the V of a red-and-black bandana kerchief covering his face from mid-nose down. On his heels came a second man, similarly garbed with a dark blue mask covering his lower face, dashing for his horse as well. The third man, also in work shirt, jeans, bandana kerchief mask (blue and white), came charging out, a six-gun in one hand and saddlebags stuffed with bank bags slung over his other arm.

The first one out never made it to his horse. York's .44 took the top of his head off, which flew away with the dead man's hat still on it. The robber fell near his horse, the animal so well-trained, so used to guns blazing, that a yawnlike whinny was its only reaction.

The second man got to his horse and on it and the animal was just about to gallop when its burden lessened, as two blasts from York's .44 caught him in the back, and he let go of the reins and fell off the saddle on the bank side of the street, but got dragged a ways before the horse, getting up a good head of steam now, broke free.

The last man, the saddlebags-turned-moneybags slung in front of his saddle's duck horn, was mounted already, York too busy killing his confederates to stop him from taking off. And while that shooting was going on, York was blocked from the third man by the two he was busy sending to hell.

Now the surviving robber was heading toward the livery, the horse already working some speed up.

That was when Sheriff Ben Wade barreled out of his office and down the steps to plant himself in the street in front of the oncoming man on horseback, the lawman taking aim with his Peacemaker. The rider swung around him but, as he did, fired once at the sheriff, with the ease of a marksman knocking a tin can off a fence post.

Then the rider was gone, cutting to the left, past the livery, where Tulley had come out with a shotgun in his hands but too late to do anything, hoofbeats receding.

The sheriff was just standing there, like he was thinking about what just happened, trying to make sense of it, weaving just a little. Then he went down all at once, like a house of twigs a child was building.

York went to the first one he'd shot, glanced down at the dead man, who was on his back with a soup of brains and blood emptied out of his ragged skull top, and kicked the weapon from limp fingers. He jogged to the other rider, the one the horse had dragged some, on his back with arms and legs going strange directions, and found the man at least as dead as his compadre, his six-gun lost in the shuffle.

Then York sprinted to Ben Wade, though he knew there was no hurry. The heavyset older man had wound up on his side, like a man sleeping who finally found a comfortable position, hat under him like an insufficient pillow. Some red had leaked from the hole in his chest across his vest and shirt and was soaking the sand, but no blood was flowing now. Dead men don't bleed.

Caleb York, the black he wore making him an instant mourner, knelt over the man he'd brought to town, to take his place, and he said a prayer for him. But at the end of it he didn't say, "Amen."

He said, "Goddamn."

God damn those who did this.

Townspeople were moving gingerly into the street, but Willa was moving quickly past the dead thieves, the bank president, and a clerk emerging with guns in hand—too little, too late—and over to York, who still knelt at his dead friend's side. She crouched near the man she loved, put a hand on his shoulder.

"Caleb, are you all right?"

"No."

"Lord! Were you hit?"

"No. But I'm not all right. I won't be till I bring in Ben Wade's killer."

York unpinned the badge from Wade's chest. Ben had said York would have to tear it off, if he wanted to take it back. But that wasn't necessary.

He stood, and Willa rose with him.

She asked, "Does that mean . . . you're staying?"

"For as long as it takes, I am."

She pinned the badge on him.

CHAPTER TWO

Ladies in gingham were letting their husbands make the journey into the sandy street, to get a closer look at the aftermath of the shooting, staying behind on the plank boardwalk soothed in awning shade.

But Willa Cullen was not some timid female. She stayed right with Caleb York as he returned to the first of the men he'd shot.

Not that she didn't find the sight grotesque—splayed out like a squashed spider, empty eyes staring up into the heaven that no doubt would be denied him, the insides of his skull emptied out like pie filling that hadn't set yet.

But a woman raised on a ranch—even a woman of a mere twenty-two years—had viewed many a gory sight before, had witnessed butchery of beef and seen men horribly injured, and by age seven had overcome any girlish queasiness of stomach. Last year, when both Trinidad and the surrounding countryside seemed littered with carnage as a result of Harry Gauge's misdeeds, she'd had her lack of squeamishness challenged, and rose to the occasion.

Still, when Caleb knelt over the corpse, Willa chose not

to kneel with him. But she did not avert her gaze when he pulled down the man's red-and-black bandana kerchief to reveal a scruffy, bearded face.

"Recognize him?" Caleb asked her, without looking her way.

"One of Harry Gauge's deputies, isn't he?"

Caleb rose and his eyes met hers. "Clay Peterson. He didn't wear a star. He worked at the Circle G."

The Circle G had been the biggest ranch controlled by Gauge, out of the seven or eight the schemer had bought up in that landgrab. The G became the corrupt sheriff's home, when he wasn't staying in town.

Caleb walked over to the second of the dead men, the one who'd been hauled by his horse a ways. One of the man's boots was gone, probably still in its stirrup, on a horse headed nowhere. He was on his back with his arms and legs going every which way. His masked face was to his left, and his torso bore two big gaping wounds, chest and stomach, scorched black and shiny red with glimpses of innards. Ranch girl Willa knew that exit wounds always looked worse than entry ones, and this crook had got two from Caleb in the back.

She asked him, "Ever shot a man in the back before?"

"Sure. That's how you stop somebody running away."

Caleb knelt over the corpse. Willa was fine just standing nearby. Didn't want to get in his way, after all. He turned the dead man's face toward him and tugged down the dark blue handkerchief mask, revealing a mustache over an open mouth showing off terrible, sporadic teeth. The dead man's face was frozen in surprise and . . . something else, what?

Disappointment.

Glancing up at her, Caleb said, "How about this one?"

"Another of Harry Gauge's bunch. Worked in town some and *did* wear a badge."

Brushing off the knees of his black trousers as he rose, Caleb said, "Len Cormack. He was working one of the spreads Gauge took over. The Running C. What do you make of it?"

"Even dead," she said, with a shudder, "Harry Gauge is bedeviling this town."

Caleb shook his head. "No, he just left a bunch of rabble behind in his wake. The kind of excuse for a man who can't earn an honest day's wage." He noticed something behind him and turned. *"Perkins!"*

The undertaker—who at the sound of gunfire could get into his black coat and black top hat so fast he might have willed it—was having his own look at the corpses. Right now this exclamation point of a man was goggling at the one with the top of his head shot off.

Caleb went over to him.

"Mr. Perkins," Caleb said sternly, "your first order of business is to get Ben Wade off the street and into your funeral parlor. The dead lowlifes can wait."

Perkins nodded. "You mind if I clean up them other two, and put 'em in my window? Good for business."

"I don't care what you do, after you done right by Ben. This one here, you'd best find his hat and the rest of his head."

"I was just thinkin' that, Sheriff."

"Just the temporary sheriff, Jacob."

"Everything's temporary in this life, Mr. York."

A group of men had gathered in the street, well-dressed, older; they included the bank president who'd just been robbed and other members of the Trinidad Citizens Committee. Normally, a gavel called such a meeting to order. Today it had been gunshots.

Seeing the men murmuring among themselves, their concern clear, Caleb called, "I've put this badge on for now—any objections?"

The city fathers glanced at each other and began exchanging head shakes that amounted to glum approval. After some low-voiced muttering, they almost shoved the mayor forward.

Jasper Hardy, the town's barber, had gained his leadership position primarily because he was the best-groomed man in Trinidad. Small, about forty, with slicked-back black hair and a handlebar mustache worthy of a picture frame, the mayor approached Caleb with halting, tentative steps.

"Mr. York . . . Sheriff York . . . would you like us to raise a posse?"

"No, sir. Thank you. Only one man escaped and only one man will pursue. Now, if you'll excuse me, I need to fetch my gun belt."

"Certainly."

Willa waited while Caleb headed back to the hotel, where his carpetbag remained. As she stood there in the street, she heard a familiar voice call out, "*Miz Cullen!* Where's Sheriff York got hisself off to? There's a *bank robber* needs catchin'."

She turned to see the supposedly reformed town drunk, Jonathan Tulley, leading Caleb's beautiful black-maned, dappled gray gelding by its reins. On the steed's back, a black well-tooled saddle awaited its rider.

"He's just gone to get his gun belt," she said. "He's going after the scoundrel, all right."

"Good! You know, he give me that Remington coach

gun of his, the other day . . . but I'm givin' it back." Tulley gestured to the double-barreled twelve-gauge shotgun already in its scabbard.

"I know he'll appreciate that, Jonathan."

Caleb was coming out of the hotel, taking the steps down to the street two at a time, buckling on his gun belt, leaving the holster tie-down loose. For now.

Seeing the saddled-up gelding waiting, Caleb grinned and he came over and patted Tulley on the shoulder, and no dust rose for a change. The old boy really had turned a new leaf, she noted—no liquor smell on him, either.

Tulley said to Caleb, "Fixed you up some jerky and a full canteen, Sheriff."

"Appreciated."

Blue eyes sparkled in the leathery bearded face. "You want me to ride along with you, Sheriff? Well, mebbe not 'along'—me and Gert can't keep pace. But we could bring up the rear."

Gert was Tulley's mule, who'd been with him going back to when his prospecting petered out.

"No thanks, *amigo*. Keep an eye on the town for me."

"Will do, Sheriff! Will do."

Before he mounted the gelding, Caleb gave Willa's hand a squeeze and her eyes told him to take care. His nod said he would, but in truth she was not much worried for this man. Yes, there was always danger, and if that robber had any sense, he'd be waiting in high rocks with a rifle to bushwhack Caleb York, because facing this man down could only end badly for the one doing it.

Caleb was barely in the saddle when bank president Thomas Carter strode up and planted himself before man-and-steed, much as Sheriff Wade had done with the fleeing bandit. In a dark gray suit and an embroidered

waistcoat, the big-framed banker made an imposing figure, his hair dark but speckled with white, mustache, too,
his chin firm if resting on a second one.

"Mr. York . . . Caleb . . . *Sheriff* . . . I'm offering you ten
percent of anything you recover. This town is depending
on you, sir."

Caleb pulled back on the reins, his horse ready to go.
"Mr. Carter, with this star on my shirt, even temporary,
any reward is improper. But you can do me one favor."

"Yes, sir?"

"Pay for Ben Wade's burial."

Men in the street parted like the Red Sea to let Caleb
on his gelding pound by, heading for the livery and making the same left turn the outlaw had.

The undertaker and an assistant were getting Ben Wade
into a wicker basket, while the townspeople were slowly
scattering and getting back to whatever they'd been
doing. Perhaps Willa should, too.

Harmon, the plump, white-bearded Bar-O cook, had
ridden in with her on a buckboard to get some supplies
from Harris Mercantile, which he was likely doing right
now, unless he'd got caught up in the rubbernecking.

So when heavyset, blond, mustached Newt Harris approached her, a man in his fifties in a medium brown suit
and dark brown string tie, she figured he was going to
tell her the buckboard was loaded, and he was due some
payment.

But it was something else.

"The Citizens Committee is holding a meeting," he
said, hat in hands, and nodded toward his store. The rear
of the place was where the group usually got together. It
was also where the circuit judge sat, as well, when the
town had one of its rare trials.

"I'm sorry, Mr. Harris," she said, "but my father didn't come into town with me today."

George Cullen was a member of the committee.

"Miss Cullen," he said, with an oddly shy smile, "it's not your father we wish to talk to. And we don't need him for a quorum. Everybody else is present. Would you please come?"

And within a very few minutes, she found herself seated at the table in the very chair where the circuit court judge usually sat, with Mayor Hardy next to her, a gavel before him. He used it to bring the meeting to order, though that wasn't necessary—the half-dozen men in chairs facing her in a semicircle sat as quiet as Sunday mid-sermon.

A wood-burning stove was to their backs, unlit, between them and the front two-thirds of the store, with its high shelved walls of goods, a pair of clerks doing their best to keep customers from being distracted by the important doings in back. Harmon wasn't among the customers, so the cook must already be loaded up and waiting.

Everything seemed very formal at first, but then the well-groomed mayor turned to her and smiled. The big mustache seemed to be its own smile.

"We'd like to ask your help, Miss Cullen."

How strange.

She said, "Anything within *reason,* Your Honor."

"Uh, that designation isn't necessary, my dear. I hope we're all friends here. All good citizens of Trinidad."

An edge of irritation made her shift in her wooden chair.

"Well," she said, "I don't live in Trinidad. I live on my father's ranch, as you well know. But I consider Trinidad my home, in a way. We do business here. We have friends. What is it you need from the Cullens?"

Skinny, bug-eyed Clem Davis, the apothecary, chimed in, "Miss Cullen, as the mayor says, it's *your* help we need. With . . . with Caleb York."

Hardware-store owner Clarence Mathers, his elaborate mutton chops seeking to make up for a lack of hair on top, said, "Not meaning to speak out of turn, young lady, but it's well-known around these parts that you carry a certain . . . influence . . . with Caleb York."

She frowned. She *did* think he was speaking out of turn.

What did they want from her?

"What we're trying to get at," the mayor said, his smile nervous now beneath the grandiose handlebar mustache, "is that we hope you will try to convince Mr. York to stay on in Trinidad."

She almost laughed, but managed to stifle it.

If they only knew . . .

"My dear," the mayor was saying, "we would like Mr. York to take on the position of sheriff on more than a merely temporary or interim basis."

"Right now," their host, Harris, said, "he's acting out of friendship and loyalty . . . and dare I say anger . . . in going after Ben Wade's killer."

"If anyone can succeed in doing that," she said, "Caleb York is the man."

"Oh, we know," the mayor said. "It brings our little community honor and even prestige to have such a stalwart figure among us—a legend who has stepped right out of the pages of the history of the West to be tiny Trinidad's representative of law and order."

He might have been making a campaign speech.

"I don't think," Willa said, and now her smile came through, "that telling Caleb York he makes a good tourist attraction is the way to convince him to stay on."

"Not our intention!" the mayor blurted. "Right now we need him, desperately, because . . . and this is not hyperbole, my dear . . . Trinidad's very existence is at stake."

Nods among the city fathers blossomed all round.

Willa was frowning. "How so?"

The men seated before her turned to the distinguished figure seated in their midst—the president of the First Bank of Trinidad, Thomas Carter.

"Miss Cullen," he said, in a rich baritone that did not diminish the devastation his expression conveyed, "that wretched bandit today made off with almost all of the cash in our vault. It represents a sizeable portion of our institution's worth, virtually everything but the building itself and, of course, what we've invested in our local businesses and the ranches around us."

His fellow committee members were glumly shaking their heads.

Carter continued: "Frankly . . . and I would appreciate it if everyone here would keep this under their hats . . . it positions the bank at the brink of failure. It's as if those blaggards had robbed each and every one of First Bank's depositors at gunpoint."

"The loss," the mayor said, "could kill our community."

The banker shook his head. "No, it *will* kill our community. There's no coming back from this, short of a miracle. That money *must* be recovered."

"Well," Willa said, "I'm sure it's Caleb's intention to do just that. This isn't merely a man seeking revenge for the death of a friend. Temporary or not, he takes that star on his chest most seriously."

A collective sigh of relief went up.

"But," she said, holding up a forefinger, "once that job

is done, Caleb York will pack up that carpetbag of his and depart Trinidad. Of that I have little doubt."

Apothecary Davis, who seemed to need one of his own calming powders about now, was half out of his chair. "You *have* to convince him, Miss Cullen! Use your feminine wiles, if needs must!"

This embarrassed everyone at the meeting, including (belatedly) Davis himself.

"Perhaps you should check at the Victory Saloon, Mr. Davis," she said coolly. "I believe you can purchase, or least *rent,* feminine wiles at *that* establishment."

"Apologies, ma'am," Davis said, hanging his head now.

Calling her "ma'am" didn't warm her to the man, either. But at least it hadn't been "madam."

The mayor said, "We have another concern, Miss Cullen, and surely it's one that has occurred to you. Your mention of the Victory Saloon brings it to mind, in fact."

She blinked at him. "It does?"

Hardy nodded.

How did that small face manage that large mustache?

He said, "We will soon have, among us, another of the Gauge clan . . . one Zachary, a cousin. From the East."

"I'm aware of that," she said. "We all are, aren't we? There's no reason to assume that Zachary will be the same kind of man as his late cousin. 'Judge not, lest ye be judged.' "

Perhaps an ill-chosen remark, Willa thought, seated as she was in a chair often occupied by a circuit court judge.

"But he may well be of that same evil stripe," Mathers said, shaking a finger worthy of a tent preacher. "And if he *is,* we face a day as dark as anything Sheriff Harry Gauge ever visited upon this town."

The apothecary spoke up again, less excited now but no less sincere. "Every one of us, Miss Cullen . . . *every one of us* . . . was in business with Sheriff Gauge. We didn't *want* to be. . . ."

"You did at first," she reminded them.

"True," Harris put in. "True enough. But Harry Gauge was a swindler. And we will be pursuing the rightful ownership of our businesses through the courts. You may be aware we hired a legal man in Albuquerque. The thing is, law or not . . . if Zachary turns out to be his cousin incarnate, we might be bullied and battered into maintaining co-ownerships that were born out of extortion."

She turned to the mayor. "Why do you mention the Victory Saloon?"

"Well," the mayor said, choosing his words carefully, "you may recall that Harry Gauge co-owned that drinking and gambling emporium with one Lola Filley."

Coldly she said, "Who died at the hands of Vint Rhomer, Gauge's number two man."

Killed by Caleb York.

"Yes," Hardy said. "But that saloon is now wholly owned and operated by her younger sister, Rita Filley. Arrived here from Houston near a month ago. I inquired personally, and Miss Filley showed me the papers. Zachary Gauge has signed the place over to her."

She thought about that. "Well, perhaps he'll do the same with the rest of the Trinidad shopkeepers. That hardly seems an indication of ruthlessness."

"I'm afraid," Mathers said, "we don't view it that way. The Gauge cousin could have shut down the place entirely. Instead he turns it over to . . . forgive me, child . . . yet another trollop. And perhaps remains a silent partner."

"A town like Trinidad," she said, "will always have a saloon. We're lucky there's only the one."

Some frowned; others nodded.

She shrugged. "These do not seem like concerns that would sway Caleb York into staying. You should discuss all of this with him, of course, and that would be a better path to take than using me as a . . . conduit, shall we say?"

She rose.

So did all the men.

"Gentlemen, you need to do your own bidding. I can't help you."

Still on their feet, the men began to murmur among themselves, much as they'd done out in the street where blood met sand.

"*However*," she said, speaking up, all eyes turning to her, "I can think of *one* possibility."

Seven men, all at once, with some overlapping, said, "Yes?"

"Caleb York has been offered a position with Pinkerton, in San Diego," she said in a matter-of-fact manner. "I would imagine many, perhaps *all*, of you know as much."

Nodding, they returned to their chairs and listened.

"Well," she said, "negotiate with the man. Ask him what they're offering, and top it. He wants respectability. Assure him you are forward-looking, that Trinidad isn't an outpost on the past, but the promise of tomorrow. They have telephones in Tombstone, did you know that? They say before long, we'll have horseless carriages. Offer Caleb York a nice house in town, as opposed to that dreary hotel room you gave him. Make the job attractive to him. Use your . . . masculine wiles."

The banker spoke up. "Miss Cullen, that will cost a small *fortune!*"

"If he brings back your money," she said, "you'll be able to afford it."

And she nodded, bid the gentlemen good day, and took her leave.

CHAPTER THREE

The sun rode high over the flat, dusty expanse beyond Trinidad, providing a nice warmth to take the edge off the day's crisp coolness as Caleb York headed out the rutted narrow road, riding hard but holding back some. Five minutes out, just past the mesquite tree-shaded cemetery called Boot Hill, despite its scrubby flatness, he had to make way for the stagecoach that he would have been on, had things gone otherwise.

He had been following the dirty cloud the fleeing bandit on horseback raised, but once the coach passed, the larger dust storm trailing it obscured that signature.

Buttes in the distance glowed a burnt red, their cliff sides wearing black scars left by wind and rain. There was a chance York's man was hiding in the mesa above those buttes, which offered up many a hiding place—boulder formations, gorges with caverns, winding arroyos. That no-man's-land was nowhere York cared to search for this human rattler, not when so many nonhuman ones lurked as well.

Anyway, the bandit wouldn't likely make that dangerous choice. A masked man need only get far enough away to change horses and maybe clothes and get all that money into a hiding place, whether a hole in the ground or a cast-iron safe. Every bank around had no-questions-asked deposit boxes. All York's man had to do was get to Ellis or Las Vegas or any number of other towns in the neighboring area, and he was home free.

Even with the Concord Coach–stirred dust, York could still keep an eye out for smaller dust storms to the left and right, which would indicate the bandit had cut off the road and gone overland, for an as-the-crow-flies route to a town or perhaps a ranch where an accomplice waited.

But York saw no indication of this all the half-hour way to the crossroads of Brentwood Junction, the relay station where stages took on fresh horses while thirsty passengers had a drink and a bite of food.

He slowed the gelding to a trot, approaching the modest cluster of weathered gray buildings—barn, corral, main building. The animal clip-clopped slowly past the wooden-fenced enclosure, where one horse stood out among the ten milling there—a black mustang.

Three such sleek black steeds had waited outside the bank as their owners made an armed withdrawal.

And this mustang, still wearing a foamy coat, its head hanging, had been ridden good and damn hard.

The rest—three chestnuts and two bays—were Morgan horses, a breed suited to stagecoaches, muscular, but not sleek like the smaller, more agile mustangs.

York pulled back the reins and climbed down from his saddle, and hitched the gelding at a corral post, rather than the hitching post across the way, outside the main relay-station building. He withdrew his .44 and moved slowly toward the shabby structure. When he stepped up onto the shallow plank porch, he did so carefully, so as not to announce himself.

But when he went through the saloon-style batwing doors, he did so quickly, gun ready, fanning it around the low-ceilinged space, short bar at left, dining tables at right, the kind of unpainted, utilitarian premises you could get away with in this part of the world.

The only person in sight was a short, skinny, mustached bartender in a black bow tie and what had once been a white apron. His hands had gone up immediately upon York's entrance, palms out, as if proving that they were clean. Which they weren't.

Those hands didn't stay up long, because the bartender—Irwin Fosler—recognized York as the sheriff of Trinidad.

York stepped inside and got a wall behind him. "You alone, Irwin?"

"Just me and Maria, Sheriff."

Maria was Irwin's plump Mexican wife, who peeked out from the kitchen in back of the bar and smiled and waved and disappeared.

York moved to the bar. "You had a lone rider."

"I did. Maybe fifteen minutes ago. Twenty minutes after the stage took off."

Hell, the bastard must have run his horse half to death.

"Did he pay you for a horse?"

"What? No."

"Then he made a trade, Irwin, and it wasn't a fair one. There's a mustang out there among your Morgans. How long was he here, that you know of?"

"Minutes. He had a shot of red-eye and skedaddled." Irwin frowned and leaned both hands on the bar. "Who was he, Sheriff?"

"A son of a bitch who robbed the First Bank of Trinidad and shot Ben Wade dead. What did he look like?"

The bartender's eyes widened. "You're lookin' for him and you don't know?"

"I know he was wearing a light blue work shirt and denims. But he also wore a mask. Anything distinctive under that mask?"

Irwin frowned in thought. "His nose was kind of on the flat side. Like it got busted more times than was helpful. He was unshaved, not like he was growin' a beard, more just scruffy-like, and there was a white scar here . . ." The bartender pointed just past and below his nose and above his lip. ". . . ran all the way down to here." He ran the finger down to just above his chin. "Knife, most probably."

"How tall?"

"How tall are you, Sheriff?"

"Six-one."

"Three inches shorter, maybe?"

"How heavy?"

"Slim. Wiry."

"Dark or pale?"

"Pale. That boyo don't work outdoors. But he was dark, far as his hair goes. And his eyes. They had a kind of sleepy look, come to think of it."

"Anything else?"

"His gun. Wore it low on the hip. So low his hand brushed it. Gunslinger maybe?"

"Bank robber surely. Thanks, Irwin."

"Don't mention it, Sheriff."

"Irwin?"

"Yes, Sheriff?"

"If you sold him a horse, say so now."

The hands came up, in dirty-palmed surrender. "I didn't, Sheriff! God is my witness! You can ask Maria. I don't own them horses, the stage company does."

A man not owning a horse didn't mean he hadn't sold it; but York didn't press the matter.

"Do they wear a brand, the stage company's horses?"

Nodding emphatically, the bartender said, "They do—BC. Bain Company."

York nodded toward the outside. "Those horses out there. Any of them fresh?"

"Team of four left by the stagecoach, anything but. The rest are daisies, Sheriff. If he unbeknownst swapped me for one, he'd have took one of them fresh ones. If he's smart at all."

"He's that smart, anyway. Thanks, Irwin."

But before he left, York held up a hand to keep the bartender back and silent, and slipped into the kitchen, gun in hand, where Maria, big breasts overflowing her peasant dress, was at the stove stirring something that smelled like a brush fire. She grinned at him, the gun not bothering her.

"You stay, *señor*? You stay and eat?"

"No thanks, Maria. Next time."

York holstered his weapon and rejoined the bartender. Dry from the ride, he took time for a beer, paying with a quarter, letting Irwin keep the change of a dime.

Outside, in the dusty courtyard between the main building and the corral, York stood with hands on hips surveying the world and his options.

With a crossroads like Brentwood Junction, there was no way to know which direction his man had gone, dust currently stirred in all four possibilities—the best of which might be Las Vegas, New Mexico, a forty-mile ride. With a train in Las Vegas, York's quarry could be long gone real soon.

He shook his head and sighed, then walked to his horse,

not as ridden-out as the bandit's but foam-flecked just the same, meaning it had been overworked. He went to the water trough, found a sponge, and took time to cool the steed down.

In fifteen minutes, man and beast were back on the rutted road, at an easy pace, heading in the direction of town.

Not all was lost. He had three ways to track the bandit now—the man was dark-haired, in his thirties, about five foot ten inches tall, with a rough beard and a scar cutting vertically through his lips; he was riding a stolen horse with a Bain stage company brand; and he had a lot of cash, which he'd likely start spending like payday at the end of a cattle drive. That smart he probably wasn't.

The scar was likely the best lead. The horse might be got rid of, and the bastard could always shave. And maybe he would know enough not to start throwing money around too damn free.

Maybe.

What York had in mind for tracking the bank robber was not a manhunt in the mountains, nor was it riding hard to Ellis and Las Vegas and every town in the territory, till his gelding dropped dead.

People thought of him as a gunfighter, and he supposed that wasn't wrong, but Caleb York viewed himself first and foremost as a detective. He had been a Wells Fargo agent long enough to know damn well that actual investigative work wasn't exciting or glamorous.

The citizens of Trinidad expected blazing guns from him, and things might well come to that; but his weapon right now was the telegraph. He would get back to town to the Western Union office and fire off not rounds from his guns, rather telegrams to every lawman in the territory, with the particulars, from scarred lip to big spending.

But he had a hunch to play first. He didn't like losing the time, but he felt the risk was worth it.

The trail that veered off to the Circle G was so narrow and rough as to make the rutted main road seem a generous ribbon of silk. The land it cut through began unpromisingly—clumped bunch grass, spiny shrubs, assorted cacti—and seemed just another stretch of desert pretending it was worth living on.

But things began to green up after a mile or so, and by the time York rode under the squared-off, fence-post gateway—a G in a circle burned in the wood overhang—his eyes were filled by a luxuriant stand of looming evergreens that lent an unlikely rustic charm to the scattering of frame structures (barn, bunkhouse, water tower, ranch house) that nestled in and around the firs. Their abundance was thanks to a nearby stream, an offshoot of the Purgatory River, which more than anything made this property desirable.

The ranch had but a single corral, though a good size one of rough-hewn fencing that looked slapped together but did the job. Within was a herd of wild horses—he counted thirteen—and four cowhands in battered hats, neck-knotted kerchiefs, and chaps over denims, trying to get a handle on their reluctant guests. Three more cowboys were on the other side of the fence, observing and offering suggestions and spitting tobacco and laughing.

The horses were running in a circle, mocking their would-be masters, two of whom had roped the same chestnut mustang and were doing everything they could to stay on their feet. Dust hung as heavy as forest-fire smoke, and the cowhands yelling at the horses and each other were all but drowned out by whinnying and neighing and pounding hooves.

Not wanting the gelding to get excitable due to all this equine activity—not that the animal had enough pep left to do anything about it—York guided it to the hitching post outside the ranch house. He twirled the reins around the post.

Somebody called out, *"York!"*

His back was to whoever had yelled. With a private smile, he plucked the sheriff's badge off his shirt and slipped it in his pants pocket.

Through the smoky fog that the horses were raising came one of the cowboys who'd been leaning against the fence on the safe side, giving pointers to those in the thick of it.

York didn't meet the man halfway—why get nearer to all that stirred dust?—and just waited until the figure became clear.

The Circle G's ramrod, Gil Willart, an average-size man with an above-average-size mustache, was heading over to him. The man wore a shapeless cowpuncher's hat with not much brim, dusty chaps over Levi's, and a brown silk shirt of the weave that kept the wind out or tried to. His eyes were green, his face oval, his skin leathery, his expression suspicious.

"Somethin' I can do for you, York?" It was a midrange voice as rough as barnwood, with a speech impediment caused by a cheekful of chaw.

"What say we go inside," York said pleasantly, "where we don't have to swallow dirt? Or listen to those fools tryin' to be cowboys?"

Willart thought about it, then shook his head. "No, out here'll have to do. We're keepin' the house spick-and-span for the new owner. Be here any day, y'know."

York nodded in the opposite direction of the corral. "Then let's take a walk."

Willart thought about that, too, then shrugged.

"Why not?" the ramrod said, and chewed tobacco as he fell in alongside his visitor.

They wound up near the water tower. A wooden bench gave them a place to sit. Now the noise of the men and horses was just far enough away to talk over.

"Quite a bunch of mustangs," York said.

"You come to jaw or is there a point?"

"Be nice, Gil. You owe me."

Willart turned his head and spat a foul brown stream. "Don't recall that I do."

York gave him an easygoing grin. "After your old boss stopped breathing, and I wore a badge for a time? I could have rounded up a posse and run all of you Gauge boys out of New Mexico."

He grunted something like a laugh. "You didn't have nothin' on us."

York turned over a hand. "Maybe not. But getting something wouldn't have been hard. All I needed was a couple of hands willin' to testify to save their skins. In that case, you would've got off easy, just gettin' run out of the territory. You and your boys rustled cattle, Gil. You mixed poxed cows with healthy ones. You were one bad *hombre,* my friend."

The cowboy spat more brown juice. "Then why didn't you come after us?"

York shrugged. "Haven't you ever heard the expression 'live and let live'?"

That grunt of a laugh again. "I heared it. But I ain't never figured it was *Caleb York's* favorite sayin'."

"Most of the outright outlaws and gunslingers—not all, but most—got out when the getting was good. Those of you who were real cowboys, and just went astray some, I figured you might wind up back on the right path." He shrugged. "This country needs good cowhands."

Willart leaned toward him, frowning, some indignation in it. "Listen, York. A cowhand's all I *ever* was. I had no part of what Harry Gauge was up to. I wasn't wise to *any* of it. Just did my job."

"Gil. You expect me to buy that?"

The bulge in his cheek was like half of him had the mumps. "How about we just say I turned over a new leaf? And leave it be?"

York pretended to consider that. "Well, maybe *before*, we could have. But the problem is, Gil . . . things have changed some."

Willart frowned again. No indignation this time. "How's that?"

"Seems we had a little trouble in town this morning."

His eyebrows went way up. "If so, word ain't got to us out here. What *kind* of trouble?"

"Three men stuck up the Trinidad bank."

Willart shot more tobacco juice to one side. "Damn shame," he said, not looking like he cared one way or the other. "What's it got to do with me?"

"Two of them got shot."

"Shot dead?"

"That's right."

His smirk was barely visible under the thick oversized mustache. "Who by? That old-time tin star you brought in to take your place? What's his name?"

"Ben Wade."

"Right. Kind of famous in his day, I hear. So . . . he shot two of 'em, huh?"

"No. They shot *him*."

Willart froze just as he was about to spit. He coughed

and swallowed some of the foul stuff, and made a face. But he said nothing.

"Well," York added, correcting himself, "*one* of them shot him. The one who got away. With all the money, as it happens."

Some panic came into the leathery face. "If you're lookin' for that one here—is *that* what you're doin', York? Lookin' for him out *here*?"

"Let's just say I'm looking for him."

Willart gestured toward the corral, where the horses were still ahead in the game.

"Well, take a look around," the ramrod said. "You see any familiar faces? Those are all top hands I hired on my own. None of 'em was even *here* six months back. They're a damn good bunch, and to a man straight as a dye. Anyways, what are *you* out doin' the lookin' for? You break off from the posse or somethin'?"

"I *am* the posse, Gil."

He frowned. "What the hell. I didn't even know you was still in town! What the hell's any of it to *you*, anyways? Ain't you headed to San Francisco or somewheres?"

"San Diego. But I decided to put that off." He reached in his pocket, got the badge out, and took his time pinning it back on.

His jaw loose, some nasty dark liquid dribbling out, Willart just stared at the tin star, like he expected it to speak.

"Thing is," York said, "those two sons of bitches I killed? Did I mention I was the one shot them? They used to work for Harry Gauge. Both of 'em. One used to work here at the Circle G, Gil. With you."

"Hell you say."

"The hell I do say. Clay Peterson. The other, Len Cormack, bunked in at the Running C. Another of your old boss's spreads."

He spat tobacco. "Well, they ain't been workin' here lately, nor at the C, neither. I knowed them two, and neither one could tell a cow from a bull. I wouldn't *have* 'em."

York was studying him. "You had Peterson when Harry Gauge was running the place."

"Now *I'm* runnin' the place."

"For your new boss. Another Gauge. Met him yet?"

Willart shook his head. "No. It's all been letters and Western Union. But he's comin' any day now, and I got high hopes. Appears to be a real straight shooter. This ain't Harry come back from the grave or nothin'. This is an honest businessman from back East, lookin' to make somethin' of the place, but who is smart enough to leave the runnin' of it to me."

York took that all in. "Businessman from back East, huh? What kind of business?"

"Not cattle!" Willart snorted a laugh. Then glumly he said, "Not that he's in the cattle business here, neither. Sheriff, we're in a sorry state at the Circle G, ever since every head of ours got destroyed 'cause of the cowpox epidemic. We got a whole lot of range and not a single damn cow."

York shrugged. "I figure you hope to buy a starter herd, maybe from George Cullen."

"We do. After the new Mr. Gauge gets here, we'll be restocking for sure. Meantime, we go out and round up them wild horses. It's somethin' to do."

"Funny coincidence."

"What is?"

"All three of those bank robbers today were riding mustangs. Handsome black devils."

Willart frowned and shook his head. "Well, them mustangs didn't come out of *that* wild bunch! That's for damn sure."

"No. They didn't. These were well-trained animals. Gunshots didn't rear 'em. That is damned unusual. This the first mustang band you rounded up?"

Willart shook his head. "Second. Sold the first off at Las Vegas. But don't get no ideas—that was just a couple weeks back, and you don't train a mustang to behave hisself in *that* time."

"No you don't." York locked eyes with the man. "Now about the man I *didn't* shoot, Gil. The one who got away with all that money?"

"What about him?"

"He's five-ten, dark-haired, flat-nosed, unshaved, pale, with a scar running through his mouth here." York indicated where. "Sound like anyone you know?"

Willart shifted uneasily on the bench. "Not someone I know. More like know *of*."

"That's a start. One of Gauge's bunch?"

The ramrod nodded. "From back in the old days, when Harry Gauge was just another outlaw."

"Don't suppose he has a name."

"Not much of one. Bill Johnson. Kinda handle a wanted man hides behind."

No argument there, York thought.

"Gil, when Gauge was still sheriff, was this Johnson playing cowhand on some spread, or maybe deputy in Trinidad?"

Willart shook his head. "No, not neither. More of a hired gun Gauge used, time to time. What I understand, the boss brought the man in when some rancher wouldn't sell out and needed persuadin'."

York's eyes narrowed; then he nodded. Patted his thighs. "Okay, Gil. That helps."

Then he rose and started back to where his gelding waited before Willart realized they were done. The cowboy caught up with York and walked along, but said nothing.

Just as York was ready to mount the horse, Willart gave him a tobacco-stained grin.

"Look, Sheriff. Way I understand it, this Zachary Gauge is foursquare. I'd be obliged if, when you meet the man, you don't say nothin' about my, uh, past . . . bad judgments."

"Isn't he aware you worked for his cousin?"

"Course he is. But I was foreman out here and he needed somebody who knew ranching and I guess I just fit the bill. But should he hear bad things, he might think twice."

York mulled it. "All right, Gil. But you need to do me a favor in return."

The ramrod spat a tobacco stream, then grinned brownly at York. Very friendly now. "I sure as hell will try, Sheriff."

York gestured vaguely. "There are still a handful of your old boss's outlaw cronies scattered around on the spreads he left behind. I assume all of the small ranches that Harry Gauge swallowed up are going to be consolidated into one big spread, under Zachary Gauge."

Willart was frowning. "What word was that? *Consolla what?*"

"Merged. Put together. Become one big ranch."

The smaller man nodded emphatically. "Oh, yeah. That's gonna happen. That *is* gonna happen."

"You figure you'll be ramrod of that big spread?"

"I surely hope so."

"If you are, Gil, you need to fire those men left over

from the previous regime. Those gunnies who don't know a bull from a cow? *Then* I'll take your new boss serious. And you."

Willart was thinking about that as York gave him a polite tip of his curl-brimmed black hat and rode off, past the corral, where the horses were still running the cowboys ragged.

CHAPTER FOUR

On the way out of town, past the church and before the cemetery, the Grange Hall sat on its own half acre, a two-story redbrick building with a first-floor overhang, a structure barely two years old.

While the Grange was home to meetings of ranchers and shopkeepers to talk over shared problems, the hall existed chiefly as a public meeting place, when matters of community import needed discussing; also, dances, amateur theatrics, and music performances were often held there.

This evening, a day after the bank robbery, the building's unpretentious interior—with its pale green walls, pounded tin ceiling, and varnished wood floor, a small stage with spinet piano at the far end—was filled to capacity with several hundred citizens and ranch folk crammed in. The unspoken rule at Grange Hall meetings was no guns, and a table near the door was temporary home to an array of rifles and gun belts. The attire was homespun, not Sunday-go-to-meeting but also not Saturday-night hoedown. This was no dance.

On the stage, the members of the Citizens Committee—the town's de facto city council—were seated in the same hard-back chairs as the attendees. In their dark suits and long expressions, they looked like a team of circuit-riding preachers prepared to give one hell-and-brimstone sermon after another.

The town's well-groomed barber mayor was at the podium, and he was gesturing with both hands to settle the restless crowd.

"We need to keep our calm, friends," the diminutive mayor said, his voice bigger than he was. "We face a situation that could mean the end of our community, if we don't stick together and weather this storm."

Only a politician who had not faced a rival candidate would have made so blunt a statement, and it was enough to sober the troubled faces into silence, for the moment anyway.

Willa Cullen, in blue-and-black plaid shirt and jeans and work boots, was seated toward the front on the center aisle next to her father. The old man sat forward, depending on his imperfect hearing to make up for his failed eyesight.

Gesturing toward the city fathers perched just behind him, Mayor Hardy said, "Now, our good friend Thomas Carter, president of the bank, has asked to speak to you regarding yesterday's tragic events."

The mayor stood away from the podium and held out a hand to bring forward the large-framed, impressive figure of the banker, who seemed almost to overwhelm the podium. Like the mayor, he had a speaking voice that could fill a room, and he did so.

"We have suffered a terrible setback in the life of our town," Carter said. "Not of the least of it is the loss of a good, brave man, who we barely had time to get to know . . . Sheriff Ben Wade."

Willa glanced across the aisle where Caleb York sat,

his expression unreadable. He wore his usual black, including a black vest, though no jacket, and the shirt lacked any fancy touches of gray, his string tie white. Arriving with no gun on his hip, he'd hung his hat when he entered the hall, and his reddish brown hair had a tousled look, reflective perhaps of a busy, even harried day.

The banker was saying, "I would like to commend Reverend Caldwell for so movingly leading us in prayer, and for sharing words of consolation and comfort. And may I say, Reverend, your graveside remembrances of the late Sheriff Wade, this morning, made a fine tribute. Now, as you know, the bank did not open today. . . ."

A wave of murmured disapproval rolled across the room, punctuated by several outbursts.

"*You don't have to tell us!*"

"*What's the damn* idea, *Carter!*"

The latter instance of public, mixed-company swearing indicated the level of concern and outrage, though summoning a few offended "*Well, I never!*" reactions from older ladies, as well as some smiles from the handful of older children in attendance.

"Closing First Bank today was not merely prudent but necessary," the banker said firmly, his chin raised. "We needed to undergo a full examination of our books and remaining funds. We were not *quite* wiped out by the thieves."

"*I'll take mine in pennies and nickels!*"

Carter ignored that. Up went his chin again. "Today I have made arrangements with my broker in Denver to divest myself of certain investments in order to have cash on hand, by the day after tomorrow."

This produced another wave of murmuring, less angry, more curious.

"A run on the bank," Carter said gravely, "could well

mean the ruination of this town. Remember that First Bank has invested in many of your businesses and ranches. *That* is where your money is. What I humbly request of you is that you continue to go about your business and allow us—as you continue to bank with us—to build up our reserve of funds."

"*What*," an angry rancher toward the back yelled, "*and let you fill your coffers till the next outlaws come along?*"

Carter raised his palms, but it was not a gesture of surrender. "Henceforth, an armed guard will be on duty at the bank during all business hours. We will be prepared, should this happen again."

The same rancher shouted, "*Why didn't you have an armed guard on duty yesterday?*"

That got the crowd going, but the banker's strong voice rode over it. "Our clerks are all armed! We have a gun at every window. But we were simply overwhelmed by a force of arms. This will *not* happen again, I promise you."

An older rancher, about halfway back, stood and asked, "*What if we don't wish to wait it out, while the town makes your bank solvent again?*"

"As I said, I have divested myself of some investments. By the day after tomorrow, anyone who wishes to close out his account can do so at twenty-five cents on the dollar."

Nobody liked the sound of that.

Half the room was on its feet, and just about the entire assemblage was shouting questions or flat-out yelling. Willa and her father were among the few merely listening. She glanced across the aisle at an equally stoic Caleb, and he gave her a little smile and shrug, as if to say, *People. What can you do?*

The hall was still ringing with discontent when the doors were flung open, as if by a gust of wind, and Willa (and everybody else) looked back amazed as a figure strode in, heading down that center aisle with purpose. He was tall, perhaps even taller than Caleb, in a black frock coat with waistcoat and black silk four-in-hand tie.

He'd been moving so quickly that Willa didn't get a really good look at this new arrival until he'd swept up to, and onto, the stage. The city fathers were frowning more in confusion than irritation at this boldness, although the bank president looked quite taken aback.

This late, dramatic arrival had a city look about him that was more than just a complexion little touched by sun; he had an air of sophistication that reminded Willa of actors she'd seen performing on stage on her visits to Denver.

The narrow oval of his face was marked by high cheekbones, his nose sharp but well-formed, his eyes wide-set under bold slashes of black brow, almond-shaped eyes so dark brown they seemed as black as his widow's-peaked, slicked-back hair. His mustache had been trimmed to a mere dark line above his expressive mouth.

Up on the stage, the late arrival was speaking in low tones, half-bowing to the Citizens Committee in apparent supplication. He had their rapt attention and any irritation was fading from their faces and a few smiles were blossoming. As he explained himself, they were nodding and gesturing toward the podium.

The bank president even put a hand on the arrival's shoulder and smiled and offered a hand to shake, which the new man did. The two stood facing each other, talking, for what seemed an eternity to all those present, but was perhaps thirty seconds, while a pin-drop silence took the hall. Finally the two men grinned at each other and shook hands again, as if both were pumping water at a well.

With considerable energy, the man in the silk tie took the podium, gripping it like a revival preacher. In a strong, clear voice, he said, "My apologies to you good people. I realize I've interrupted an important meeting, but when I learned what you've been put through, and what you're *going* through, well . . . I thought you might like to hear a few encouraging words . . ."

He flashed a winning smile.

". . . to invoke a familiar song that's no doubt been sung in this very building any number of times."

That same rabble-rousing rancher in back, unimpressed, called, *"Just who* are *you, mister?"*

"My name is Gauge," he said. "But I hope you won't hold that against me."

Another wave of murmuring rolled through the room.

"I only met my late and apparently very unlamented cousin a few times," he said. "When we were both young and innocent . . . though I seem to recall him setting a cat's tail on fire, so perhaps he never was."

This got some smiles and a few chuckles.

"I am Zachary Garland Gauge, and I rode here on horseback today from Las Vegas, where I arrived by train. Though I'm from the East, I do have some equestrian training. . . ." Seeing some confused faces, he rephrased it. "I've done my share of horseback riding, although I think today I earned myself a few blisters in brand-new places."

More chuckles, but many wary expressions.

His smile exuded confidence. "I hope we'll be friends soon. We're already neighbors, as I've moved in, out at the Circle G, or am in the process thereof. Several townspeople were good enough to be waiting for me when I arrived, and they let me know in no uncertain terms about the nasty blow your community's been dealt. I'm here to put your minds at ease. Before I came West, to take over my cousin's ranch, and to build a new life for myself, I liquidated all of my holdings."

Murmuring rose to a rumbling, as if an earthquake were coming.

Zachary Gauge's strong voice rose over the rumbling and quelled it: "*Please!* Gentle people. I have only had a few moments to discuss this with Mr. Carter. Just now. Obviously we will need to spend time in discussion and negotiation, at far more length . . . but your bank president assures me that the amount of money I will be depositing with him in the coming few days exceeds the losses of the recent robbery by a good distance."

A stunned silence held for several seconds; then someone started to clap and it built into applause that rang off the tin ceiling, with some whoops and hollering mixed in.

"I hope to get to know all of you better," Zachary said, and he turned to the city fathers and went down the row of them—they were on their feet now—shaking hands. Then he faced the crowd and summoned a shy smile and waved a little, as he stepped off the stage and went down the aisle, as smiling faces turned his way, words of welcome flung toward him, hands extended for quick shakes, the applause continuing. Finally the unexpected town savior took a place along the wall in back, since no chairs were left.

The committee members on stage were all seated again, save for the mayor, who again stepped to the podium. The applause finally died down and the little barber spoke.

"We are all as grateful as we are surprised," Mayor Hardy said, "to enjoy this last-second rescue, right out of a dime novel."

That got some laughter, perhaps more than it deserved, thanks to the suddenly elevated mood.

"Speaking of dime novels," Hardy said, his own mood

brightened considerably, "our own Sheriff York, the subject of such writing himself, has requested a few words with you. Afterward, we ask you to move your chairs to the sides of the hall, as the ladies of the Grange are going to serve some refreshments. . . . Sheriff York?"

Caleb rose from his chair and stepped up onto the shallow stage. He did not take the podium but rather stood near the edge of the platform and spoke words that somehow seemed quiet, though his voice was as loud as any that had spoken this evening.

"I bid welcome to Mr. Gauge," Caleb said, "and commend his investment in our community."

Willa felt a wave of warmth at Caleb referring to Trinidad in such a manner. A man staying only temporarily might not refer to the town in that way.

"But it remains my aim," he said, "to recover the stolen money and bring Ben Wade's killer to justice."

A man in back called, *"Fill him with lead first, Caleb!"*

That old-fashioned lingo got some laughs and scattered applause, but York, stony-faced, only raised a hand, as if being sworn in to testify.

"I hope to bring him in breathing," their sheriff said. "But if a jury so rules, I will gladly walk him to the gallows."

Almost everyone in the room applauded that.

That same grouchy rancher in back called out, *"Sheriff! Why didn't you raise a posse? Why aren't you out lookin' for this mudsill!"*

No one seconded that, but everyone looked Caleb's way just the same.

"That's Barney Wright, isn't it? Barney, your name may be Wright, but you have a wrong way of looking at things."

Some chuckles.

"Or at least an old-fashioned one," Caleb said. "I rode out yesterday to Brentwood Junction. Our wanted man stole a fresh horse there, and what direction he rode off in, I couldn't venture a guess. I did get a description of him. . . ."

Caleb shared that with the hall.

"I also got a name," he said. "Bill Johnson. Darn common and a likely alias. He was a crony of Mr. Gauge here's late cousin, but he didn't work on any of the Gauge spreads. Just a hired gun brought in to intimidate when needed. If any of you know of a Bill Johnson, see me after."

He explained to the crowd that he had spent yesterday afternoon sending telegrams to lawmen all over the territory and a few beyond, with the description of this Johnson, and that he'd wired the Santa Fe Railroad with the same information, so their "train dicks" would be on the alert.

"Nothing's come of this effort yet," Caleb told them. "But my investigation continues."

Then he thanked everyone for their attention, and stepped back down off the stage and returned to his chair. Once again, murmuring took the hall, as the sheriff's disappointing news seemed an anticlimax after the boost of Zachary Gauge's message.

The mayor resumed the podium to remind the group that refreshments were about to be served. Several husbands who'd been recruited set up long tables in front of the stage as their wives came out from the kitchen with twin bowls of punch and several plates of gingersnaps, then on a second trip adding cups and small plates. About half of the attendees filed out, but the others moved their chairs, and any abandoned ones, off to either side, and an area between was left for socializing.

Little groups of men formed to palaver and the women did the same, although some of the latter took the chairs that now lined the walls, sipping their punch, nibbling on cookies. Clearly, the Citizens Committee had been hopeful they could turn around this meeting about Trinidad's dire circumstances by way of the banker's assurances and a few refreshments, as if it were just another social.

That might have been wishful thinking, had it not been for Zachary Gauge's surprise appearance.

Willa, interested in neither punch nor gingersnaps, nonetheless took one of the chairs, sitting her father down next to her. She knew he felt uncomfortable standing in a room with conversation coming at him from all sides.

Moving toward them through the crowd, slender as a knife blade despite broad shoulders, Zachary Gauge came walking their way. Various men tried to stop and talk to him, and he politely nodded and informed them he'd catch up with them later. He would not be dissuaded from his goal, which appeared to be Willa and her father.

He positioned himself in front of them with a somber expression and lowered his head in something that merged a nod and a half-bow.

"Miss Cullen. Mr. Cullen. I hoped I might pay my respects."

George Cullen didn't have to be told who was standing before him—the voice he'd heard earlier was now unmistakable.

"Mr. Gauge," Papa said somewhat gruffly. "Fine words. I hope your actions meet up with them."

"May I sit, Mr. Cullen?" he asked, gesturing toward the empty chair next to her father, his eyes asking Willa the same question. She nodded and so did Papa.

Seated next to the blind man, turning toward him,

Zachary Gauge said, "I am heartsick over what I have heard, regarding the indignities my cousin visited upon you both. I can't offer an apology for the actions of a relative I barely knew. But I can assure you that while I may share the scoundrel's bloodline, I am of another breed entirely."

The rather strained formality of that might have amused Willa, had she not sensed something genuine behind the too carefully chosen, perhaps overly rehearsed words.

"Mr. Gauge," her father said, turning to cast his milky gaze on the man, "I judge men by their own deeds, not those of their family members. Who among us does not have a wayward relation?"

"I am most relieved to hear that, sir. And please—call me 'Zachary.' The Gauge name is not one viewed kindly in this community, a sentiment I wholly understand."

"You are most welcome here, sir." No gruffness now.

Her father held out his hand and Zachary shook it, smiling big.

"You're very generous, Mr. Cullen."

Papa said, "It took mettle for you to approach my daughter and me, Mr. Gauge . . . Zachary. Not every man might have the sand."

Willa said, "Father . . . perhaps Mr. Gauge—"

"Zachary," the newcomer insisted.

"Perhaps," she began again, "Mr. Gauge understands that the two biggest landowners in the area ought to get to know each other."

Zachary gave Willa a smile that fairly twitched with amusement. "Your daughter displays both rare beauty and a keen intelligence, Mr. Cullen . . . or may I call you 'George'?"

" 'George' is fine," Papa said.

THE BIG SHOWDOWN   59

"Well, Miss Cullen is right," Zachary said. "We need to cooperate and help each other."

Willa said with a smile, "I believe you need *our* help more than we do yours."

Zachary gave her another half bow, half-nod, returning the smile. "Undoubtedly, Miss Cullen. I am, as they say, land rich but cattle poor. This is something I hope we can discuss . . . though tonight is obviously not the time or the place."

"Once you've settled in," Papa said, "feel free to call on us. We'll talk business."

"Where I come from," Zachary said, "it's impolite to just drop in on people."

Papa pawed the air. "Well, around here we don't stand on ceremony. But if you'd like to set a time . . . ?"

"I would. Is around two o'clock tomorrow afternoon suitable?"

Papa nodded. "It is."

Zachary rose, said, "Thank you, sir," then smiled and nodded to Willa, saying, "Miss Cullen."

"Mr. Gauge. Zachary."

The tall man turned and almost bumped into Caleb, who had approached when they were talking, though keeping a respectful distance. Now the two tallest men in the room stood facing each other.

Caleb gave Willa a nod, and said, "Good evening, Mr. Cullen," and Papa responded similarly.

Knowing full well that father and daughter were well within earshot, Caleb began a friendly if guarded conversation with Zachary Gauge.

Offering a hand to shake, which Zachary accepted, Caleb said, "Welcome to Trinidad. You've already done the impossible."

"And what would that be, Sheriff York?"

"Made a man named Gauge the most popular person in town."

"Sheriff," Zachary said, with a good-natured smile, "I am only trying to make up, in a small way, for what the black sheep of our family visited upon this community."

"Like Mr. Cullen says, that's generous. Particularly since you and your cousin barely knew each other. And yet you're his sole heir, I understand."

"Sheer happenstance. Rights of the survivor. And I don't mean to suggest that I'm performing good deeds strictly to make amends for the sins of a cousin. Trinidad represents a real business opportunity for me . . . even if I *am* a cattle rancher without cattle."

"Property is power, in this country," Caleb said. "I have a hunch you're a man who can overcome a small detail like no cattle."

"Well . . . thank you. I guess. If I might ask . . . ?"

"Ask away."

The newcomer cocked his head. "I was given to understand that you were leaving this community."

"That was my intention. It still is."

Willa, listening, frowned.

Zachary asked, "Then this sheriff who was killed—Ben Wade?"

"Ben Wade."

"He was a friend?"

"I got him the job."

"And you're taking his place until you've tracked down his killer?"

"That's the intention. And I'd like to get that money back, too."

"The bank's money, yes."

"It's not really the bank's money. It's the people of Trinidad who *really* got robbed."

Zachary nodded twice. "Quite right. Well, if there's anything I can do to be of assistance, in your efforts, please don't hesitate to ask."

Caleb stood with hands on hips. "Well, there *is* something. I'd appreciate you taking a good hard look at the men working for you on the spreads you've inherited."

Zachary raised a palm. "Oh, I intend to. I'll be taking a hard look at all my personnel. I'll be combining those properties into one bigger ranch. Only makes sense. More efficient. I'm no rancher, not yet, but *that* much I know to do."

Caleb's eyes narrowed. "What I'm referring to, Mr. Gauge—"

"Please. 'Zachary.' "

" 'Zachary,' " Caleb said with a nod. "What I'm referring to are the outlaws still working those spreads. Hard cases mixed in with cowhands, brought in by your late cousin. Not many of them, at this point. But your ramrod, Gil Willart, should be able to single them out."

"I can assure you, Sheriff—"

"Make it 'Caleb,' Zachary."

"Caleb. I can assure you that I want nothing to do with such wastrels. They will be sent packing."

"Good. Good to hear." Caleb nodded again. "Best of luck to you in this new line of endeavor, Zachary. What was it you did back East, anyway?"

"Stockbroker, actually."

"Well. With some luck, you'll be dealing with stock again. High stakes, but spelled different."

Zachary got the joke right away.

"Well put, Sheriff. Caleb." Zachary narrowed his eyes

now. "But these outlaws—rather than just discharge them . . . wouldn't it be better if I let you know who they are, and which spread they're working? So you could talk to them personally, perhaps in regard to the bank robbery?"

"Oh, they'll stop in town at the Victory—that's our local drinking and gambling emporium—before they hit the trail. I'll have a chance to talk to all of them."

Caleb gave one more nod to the newcomer, then bid Willa and her father good night, indicating he knew full well they'd heard every word of the conversation.

Willa told her father she'd be just a minute and followed Caleb. He was out front in the cool night air, snugging on his hat, as attendees were gradually leaving, unhitching horses, climbing up into buggies.

"Is that how you behave?" she asked him, meaning it to sound strong but knowing it came out snippy.

"How is that?"

"You just say good night and walk away from me."

"I figured you were tending to your father. Or maybe to that Zachary character."

"What?"

He grinned at her. "He's already taken a shine to you. Or maybe it's your father's cattle. Or his land?"

"Are you jealous, or just a boor?"

The words seemed to soften him, or maybe that was embarrassment.

"Sorry," he said. "I have no right. And, anyway, he was probably just being polite."

"Oh, so you don't think another man might be attracted to me?"

"I think any man possessed of his senses would be attracted to you, Willa Cullen. But me? I don't have that right. Not anymore."

"And why is that?"

"You know why."

"I don't. I honestly don't."

"Because I'm still leaving Trinidad."

"What?"

He gestured vaguely toward town. "When this bank robbery case is settled, I'll be on my way. To San Diego."

He told her good night again, and walked off, while she stood there in front of the Grange Hall, fuming.

CHAPTER FIVE

At just after nine P.M., Trinidad's Main Street was uncommonly busy—buggies and men on horseback, couples strolling along the boardwalk—as those who'd attended the meeting at the Grange Hall made their way home.

But one person Caleb York had not expected to run into was his rambunctious friend Tulley, who was pacing outside the hotel entrance like an expectant father near a bedroom where a midwife was doing her work. The skinny coot lit up like a jack-o'-lantern when he spotted York.

"Git yer gun," he said, eyes wild. "Git yer damn *gun*!"

York pushed his hat on the back of his head and regarded his friend. "Any special reason?"

The white-bearded, bowlegged Tulley looked around for eavesdroppers, then leaned in. "We need to talk private."

"Well, let's go down to the office, then. I have my gun belt locked up there. Since you want me to 'git' it."

Tulley closed an eye and raised a finger. "I do, and it'll be right handy, bein' down at that end of the street and all."

"Why's that?"

The bandy-legged character took York by the arm, virtually escorting him along the boardwalk. "Too many townsfolk out tonight. This is not talk for sharin'. Meantime, on the way, you can tell me all about that Grange meetin'."

York did.

Frowning as they walked along, Tulley asked, "What do ye make of this latest branch of the Gauge tree?"

"Nothing like his cousin. Certainly talks a good game. And there's no question he's bailing out this community when it can damn well use it."

Tulley was shaking his head. "Never trust a city slicker, says I."

York grinned over at him. "Why, Tulley? How many have you run into, in your day?"

"Plenty! More'n one!"

When they got to the office, York unlocked the door and went in, Tulley trailing. The sheriff got behind his desk and lit the lamp there, suffusing the austere room with a warm yellow glow. He gestured for Tulley to pull up a chair, which the old boy did, sitting so close and leaning over so far, he all but climbed onto the desktop.

"Okay, Tulley," York said with a patient smile. "I think it's safe to talk now. Unless you'd like to check under the desk and maybe back in the cells."

Tulley paid the sheriff's joshing no heed. "You *tol'* me to keep my ear to the ground. I been doin' exactly that, purt' near all day."

"At the stable? Little messy for that."

"I didn't go in today but for a tiny bit, first thing. Told Clem I had official sheriffin' business to see to."

York was still smiling. "Aren't you afraid your work will pile up?"

"You ain't takin' me serious, Sheriff. But you should.

You will. Listen here. I was over to the cantina tonight and I seen two of Harry Gauge's gunhand cowboys, hittin' the tequila hard, and a couple of them powdered-up *señoritas* hangin' on 'em like vines on a wall."

York sat forward, smile gone. He'd told Zachary Gauge that any of the outlaws the new rancher might boot off his spreads would surely stop by the Victory Saloon before leaving town. But York had overlooked the Cantina de Toro Rojo. Few gringos frequented the joint, the clientele chiefly Mexican cowboys who worked ranches in the area, and the half-Mexican/half-Indian hands, too, and maybe some other thirsty, randy males from Trinidad's small barrio itself, home mostly to servants and laborers around town.

But hard cases like those outlaws the late Harry Gauge had taken on at his ranches would feel right at home in a deadfall like the Cantina de Toro Rojo.

"You know these men by name, Tulley?"

"I surely do. Ray Pruitt and Eli Hoake."

Both men had their faces on wanted posters, York knew, just not in New Mexico. They were accused of robbing a stagecoach in Arizona and killing the driver.

"That ain't all, Sheriff. I heard 'em talkin'. I didn't catch much . . . if I got any closer to 'em they might got wise . . . but they both said the name 'Bill' a bunch of times, and was laughin' and laughin' and tossin' back the tequila like water."

"Lot of Bills in this world, Tulley."

"How many that was on Harry Gauge's payroll?"

York thought about that, then asked, "Speaking of tossing back the tequila, Tulley, how much went down *your* gullet?"

The old boy crossed his heart right by a frayed blue suspender. "Nary a drop. I been on the water wagon for months now, Sheriff. You know that. All I put down me was some of that brown gargle them Mexies claims is coffee."

York leaned back in his hardwood chair, its front legs off the floor, and studied his friend. Maybe Tulley still sounded like a half-crazed prospector who'd just climbed down off a mountain after living alone too long; and there seemed no danger of the man losing his position as town eccentric. Yet he *had* changed. Those eyes were no longer rheumy, but as clear a blue as the best New Mexico sky, minus any clouds.

"Tulley, how are you with a handgun?"

"Slow as molasses, Sheriff, but I know which end to point. Scattergun is more to my temperament."

York waved a vague hand. "There are three in the gun rack. Pick any one you like."

Tulley frowned in confusion. "Right generous, even for Caleb York. But it ain't my birthday. Truth be told, I don't even know *when* my birthday is."

York shrugged. "Christmas is just a few months off. Call it an early present. Here's another. . . ."

He opened a desk drawer and fished around and came back with a badge that said DEPUTY. Like a bet he was making, he shoved it across the desk at the old boy, whose eyes widened. Tulley reached for it, but his fingers merely hovered, as if the badge were a hot stove.

"Merry Christmas, Tulley. Or would you rather keep shoveling horse manure over at the livery?"

"Oh, I had my fill of that, Sheriff. Even only workin' them half days."

Those added up to thirty hours a week.

"You're making, what, Tulley? Three dollars a week?"

"In that there neighborhood."

"I'll tell the Citizens Committee I require a deputy and

ask for forty a month. How does that neighborhood sound?"

Tulley was beaming. "Like I died and went to heaven. Only I don't suppose you need a scattergun up there." He reached for the badge and pinned it on the pink of his BVD top.

As he was doing that, though, his expression dropped.

"Are you *sure* about this, Sheriff? You know half of this town sees me as a joke, and the other don't see me a'tall."

"With that badge, Tulley—assuming you stay on the wagon—they'll respect you, all right."

"What if . . . what if they don't?"

"That's what the scattergun is for."

York reached in his pocket and dug out a quarter eagle, then tossed it on the desk, where it rang and shuddered before settling down.

"Get yourself a real shirt or two, Tulley, over at the mercantile. You'll get took more serious than in that underwear top."

Tulley grinned and snatched up the coin. For a reformed desert rat, he had a surprising number of teeth. "When do I start?"

"Right now."

York unlocked his right-hand bottom drawer and got out his gun belt. He stood and buckled it on, positioning the .44 butt at pants pocket level, then cinched the holster tie.

"You know that expression, Tulley—'hold down the fort'? Well, this is the fort. Hold it down till I get back."

"Will do," Tulley said, already on his feet and over at the weapons rack, selecting a shotgun.

At the door, York paused to look back and say, "Get some coffee going and unlock a cell door. Key ring's on the wall, there."

"We takin' on some new lodgers?"

"Might."

The night had grown cooler, and the street was empty, everybody home now after the gathering at the Grange. The only exceptions were the Victory, spilling its light and gaiety into the street some ways down, and of course the Cantina de Toro Rojo, over at the dead end of the ragtag collection of a dozen or so low-slung adobe-brick buildings opposite the sheriff's office and jail.

During the day, the modest barrio was that peculiar south-of-the-border mix of sleepy and lively, people in loose clothing seeming in no hurry but always caught up in some activity, chickens wandering the dusty space between the facing adobes, dogs barking and scrounging. At night, the animals were sleeping, the fowls penned up, the dogs finding doorways to curl up in, the only human inhabitant in sight a drowsy old man skirting a broken-down cart to get to an outhouse.

Down at the end of this shabby lane of yellow hovels was a two-story exception, grand by way of comparison, windows glowing yellow on the first floor, flickering candlelight in some second-floor windows. Adobe, like its neighbors, but more sturdy-looking, its architecture not so haphazard, the structure might have been a castle with peasants at its feet, or the home of the only rich man in town, or perhaps a military fortress.

This was a fortress, all right, but a fortress of sin, with big faded-red lettering above an arched doorless door saying CANTINA DE TORO ROJO. Right now the town gunsmith, in the same suit he wore to church, was coming out beneath those weather-worn letters; he was on the arm of a slender señorita with enough paint on her almost-pretty face to make her look older than she was. Old as fourteen, maybe.

The pair went up an exposed wooden staircase along the right side of the building, to the second floor—there was no access from the restaurant and bar below. Laughter and talk leached out the place, accompanied by guitar. Half-a-dozen horses stood at the leather-glazed hitch rail, tails twitching away flies. York checked for a Morgan horse with a BC brand.

Nope.

He entered the cantina, boots crunching the straw on the floor. The joint was doing a pretty fair weeknight business. The smell of refried beans hung heavy, but nobody was eating. This time of evening, the Red Bull was all about drinking and maybe going outside and upstairs with a señorita. A little guy in a sombrero too big for him sat in a corner smoking an ill-made cigarette as he played an approximation of flamenco guitar on a cheap-looking instrument.

The bartender—who was also the owner—was fat and sweaty, his round head striped with thinning black hair, his eyes hooded, his mustache droopy, his white shirt damp, his black string tie limp, his unhappiness about this new arrival unmistakable; he was pouring somebody, maybe himself, a shot of tequila.

The walls had been painted a redundant yellow a long time ago, with touches of bright colors that had faded to pastels. One wall had a surprisingly well-done mural of a bullfight, also faded. No stools at the bar, just a scattering of mismatched tables and chairs, as if assembled from furnishings that fell off wagon trains rolling through.

A few areas were partitioned off with latticework, and a handful of gringo men from town were mixed in with

Mexican cowboys who worked spreads in the area, including the Cullen ranch—such vaqueros were among the best hands in the territory.

Pruitt and Hoake, the cowboys with the stagecoach-robbery pedigree, were playing cards with two of the Mexican ranch hands. Stud poker. Coins and a few bills littered the table. Two señoritas in their twenties, with eyes in their forties, displayed a lot of dark hair, white teeth, and bosoms overflowing peasant blouses, their full black skirts with petticoats circled with occasional stripes of color—red, green, yellow, white.

The Mexicans were real cowboys, on the small side, which was the standard, since ranchers didn't like putting a strain on their horses. Tow-haired Pruitt and especially dark-haired Hoake were wrong for the job, Pruitt tall and sturdy, Hoake just shy of fat.

Both men wore denims, knotted neck kerchiefs and work shirts, as if that would fool anybody. The Colt .45s in their oiled leather holsters, tie-downs loose, told a different story. The tall half of the pair had a goatee, while the almost fat one's pie-pan face made a home for a mustache as droopy and black as the bartender's.

York went to the bar where that shot of tequila was waiting for somebody to drink it. So he did. The stuff went down with a nice burn, but tasted like it came into the world this afternoon, all cactus and no wood.

"Sheriff," the bartender said softly, "you know we like be your good neighbor."

"And your idea of a good neighbor," York said, "is me not dropping by?"

"You don't boost my patrons' thirst."

"Sure I do, Cesar. When I leave."

"So please do." A request, not a threat.

York gave the barest head nod toward the poker table. "Those fellas over there. The *gringos,* the tall, the squat? How drunk are they?"

"Not very. They take in plenty, but they do it slow. Steady. Since before sundown. They been upstairs once already. Now, I think they just try and . . ."

"Regroup their troops?"

He shrugged wide shoulders. "They been here before. They know to go upstairs, early. Pretty soon, they go upstairs maybe with a different girl, this time usually stay the night. But, uh, Sheriff, they cause no trouble."

"See any other *gringo* with them?"

"Did not notice."

"A man with a scar through his mouth? Scar standing out white against a beard? Not a big man. Slim but looks like he can take care of himself?"

"No bell rings."

"Name of Bill Johnson."

"That's a John Smith, Juan Garcia name."

"It sure is. Cesar, you wouldn't be forgetting 'cause you don't want any trouble here?"

"Not so, Sheriff. I am a good neighbor."

"Or maybe you got paid to forget?"

Cesar frowned and said, "No, *señor.* I don't need that kind of money. I make plenty here in my honest business."

"Then you don't want to get closed down."

"I do not, Sheriff." Cesar poured another tequila, but York ignored it. "There was a Bill Johnson, I think, last year. Who would come in, time to time."

"Is that right? With a scarred lip?"

"I think his lip, it is scarred. Now that I think on it."

"Why don't you drink some of that tequila, Cesar, and think on it some more."

Cesar did.

York waited.

Then very quietly, the bartender said, "I have not seen him tonight. Bill Johnson. I speak truth."

"Okay."

Glancing at the poker table, seeing no eyes on him, Cesar said quietly, "But he always like one of my girls. Gabriella."

"She working tonight?"

"*Sí.*"

"Your girls, do they use any available room, or do they have rooms of their own?"

"Of their own, *señor.*" He glanced at the ceiling. "Gabriella? First door on your left."

"Locks on the doors?"

Cesar smiled slyly. "Sheriff, if you wish to know more about such rooms, there are girls here, they be glad to give you lessons. No charge."

York grinned. "That good a neighbor I don't need you to be, Cesar. Just tell me if that door is going to be locked."

A shrug, a shake of the big head. "There are no locks in this part of town, *señor.* We are poor but honest people."

Cesar and his wife didn't live in the barrio. They had a former hacienda outside town a few miles. But York thought pointing this out might be unkind.

"Appreciate your help, Cesar. Now don't get jumpy, *amigo.* But I'm going over to say hello to those *gringos.* Then make a show of leaving."

Cesar nodded and went off to find a glass to polish. Or maybe just to wipe dry, since York had never seen him wash any.

York crossed the straw-covered floor and stood near the small table where the latest round of stud was going.

Fat Hoake looked up over his greasy cards and asked, "You want dealt in, Sheriff? It's a small-stakes game. But we play it like it matters."

The two señoritas were looking York up and down the way some men did good-looking women.

York said, "Just need a friendly word with you, Mr. Hoake. You, too, Mr. Pruitt."

Looking at his cards, sitting near where York stood, Pruitt—a moist cigarette hanging so low his goatee might have caught fire—said, "Can't this wait, Sheriff? We got a game here."

"Please. Finish the hand."

They did.

"You boys know a Bill Johnson?"

Hoake's smiling words made his droopy mustache dance. "I think I know two, no *three*, Bill Johnsons, Sheriff. Maybe you can narrow it down some."

While Hoake was looking right at York, Pruitt gazed straight ahead, sullen as hell.

York said, "You'd know this Johnson by the scar through his mouth."

Hoake pretended to think. Pruitt didn't bother.

"You'd also know him because, like you fellas, he was one of Harry Gauge's men. Oh, not *cowboys* like you two. More a . . . special deputy."

Hoake's eyebrows went up; they looked like they were pasted on the flat, round face. "Oh. *That* Bill Johnson. What about him?"

York didn't answer the question. Instead, he asked the tall outlaw, "How about you, Mr. Pruitt? You acquainted with this particular Bill Johnson?"

Now Pruitt turned to look up at York. His eyes were small and a light brown, like tobacco juice with plenty of spit in it. "We met. Ain't seen him in some time. Why?"

"You boys must not get around. I thought everybody in the territory knew by now that Johnson's wanted for robbing the First Bank of Trinidad. Got away with a hefty sum."

"Do tell," Pruitt said, those tiny eyes getting even tinier as they disappeared into slits.

"There's a reward," York said, "should you run into him. Or should it occur to you where I might find him."

One of the Mexican cowhands at the table asked, "How much reward, Sheriff?"

"Ten percent of whatever's recovered."

Hoake said, "Well, what if somebody hauls Bill Johnson in, but nothing's recovered?"

York fanned a big smile around the table. "I'm sure you would have the gratitude of your fellow good citizens. Maybe get a piece of paper from the mayor to hang on the bunkhouse wall."

Pruitt and Hoake smirked at each other.

York said, "I'll be in my office first thing tomorrow morning, gents, should something come to you. After I get a good night's sleep, anyway."

He summoned a yawn and stretched some.

"Enjoy your game, fellas."

He nodded to them, tipped his hat to the señoritas, who gave him looks about as subtle as a mule kick in the tail, then sauntered out. He walked back through the sleeping barrio and across to the office/jail and went inside.

Tulley, seated at the little table by the stove and wall of wanted posters, swung the scattergun toward him, then backed it right off.

The deputy said, "I don't see no customers."

"I'm just making a show of it," York said, and he cracked the door and peered across the street. The cantina was too far away to tell whether one or both of the gunhands had followed him to the door to watch him go. Had he looked back, he'd have tipped his hand.

But he felt sure they had. One of them, at least.

Tulley watched in confusion as York removed his spurs and tossed them on the desk with a jangle.

"You're gettin' ready for bed or somethin'?"

"In a way," York said. He grunted a laugh. "Spurs are fine on horseback, Tulley, but they have a bad habit of announcing you, on foot."

He waited five minutes before heading back. This time not even a dog barked and nobody was heading to the outhouse. Laughter and talk and guitar again welcomed his approach, without yet noting his arrival. The same horses were hitched outside the Red Bull.

York walked around to the side of the building where that exterior staircase took you closer to heaven and right next to earthly delights. Playing a hunch, he moved around back and found a lone horse hitched to a post.

A Morgan horse, a bay, with a BC brand on its right rump.

York smiled to himself and withdrew his .44.

He went over and glanced around front to see if any patron happened at that moment to be heading outside with a señorita in tow (or the other way around), and saw no one. He considered peeking in a front window to check on the card game, or at least establish the continued presence of Pruitt and Hoake, but decided against it.

Why risk being seen?

He started up the rough-wood stairway, taking each step slow and careful, unable to do so silently but not making a racket, anyway. He paused at the landing, helped himself to several slow breaths, in and out, in and out, then stood there taking in the stars for a mite, then went in taking only the star on his chest with him.

The hallway was narrow. Three staggered doors on either side, more yellow pueblo walls, a wooden floor that had been there forever and was still waiting to be swept.

"First door on your left," Cesar had said.

Did he trust Cesar?

Did he have any choice?

He turned the knob and began to push through, but—though the door, as promised, had no lock—a chair was propped under its knob. York had to back up and shoulder through, aware that he'd been announced far louder than his spurs might have, and he dove in, past the chair he'd dislodged as bullets blasted over him, three shots separated only by the click of cocking, cutting through the shrill immediate female scream that filled the room like a train whistle.

York—down on the filthy floor next to an ancient iron bed, knowing a woman was in the room with Johnson and not wanting to fire blindly—aimed up and then, leaning over him, there the man was, scar through his bearded face and his lips, bare and hairy and sinewy, eyes big, teeth bared, his Colt .45 swinging down at the man on the floor.

But the man on the floor fired just once, and the bullet went in right under the scarred gunman's nose, adding a ragged red oversized nostril just below and between the other two, and the .44 slug traveled at an angle that cut its passage through the naked man's head and sprayed the yellow ceiling scarlet with dripping dabs of green and gray. The Colt clunked to the floor, released by unfeeling fingers, and the now blank-eyed bank robber fell back onto the bed, out of York's sight.

She was still screaming, the live naked woman under the sheet with the dead naked man, looking at her bed mate but not wanting to, frozen but wishing she could move, as if a hole to hell had opened up before her and something in her wanted to dive in even as the rest of her wanted to flee.

This was Gabriella, and as close to Gabriel as Bill Johnson would ever get. She was young, though had just grown much older, a pretty thing with lots of bosom and a general plumpness that would have been more pleasing not flecked with red.

Already on his feet, York went to a second chair, which with a small table with basin represented the only other furnishings in the small room, and plucked a thin pink-and-white floral robe. His gun in one hand, he took the flimsy garment and held it out to her.

"Find another room up here," he advised her. "One that isn't being used."

She stopped screaming, swallowed, nodded, got her limbs working, and climbed off the bed and ran out, grabbing the robe from him and flashing full, dimpled buttocks as she did.

York quickly checked the room.

On the floor, spilled from the chair that had been propped against the door, were the dead man's clothes. Two hundred dollars, cash money, were in his Levi's. A closet held only the girl's red dress and white peasant blouse, plus some underthings and sandals.

He left the room, noting the three pocks in the adobe wall, holes that might have been in him. Out on the landing, in cool air under the stars again, he was about to holster his .44 when he saw them coming around from in front of the cantina, Pruitt and Hoake, their guns in hand, Colt .45s like Johnson's. Still time for York to get holes punched in him tonight.

They were aiming up at him but by the time they started shooting, standing side by side at the foot of the outdoor steps like a two-man firing squad, he was halfway down the steps, their rounds flying over him, shattering the night but nothing else, his gun raised hip-high but aiming down. He fired four times, hitting them only twice, one each, Pruitt in the left eye and Hoake in the forehead.

Not bad, considering the frantic circumstances.

He paused two-thirds of the way down as the two men staggered on dead feet, then fell together, propping each other up for a moment, almost comically, before tumbling to the ground in an awkward embrace of lifeless arms and legs. A good deal of what had been in their heads had sprayed out the back and onto the dusty ground, like a spilled plate of cantina chow.

He stepped over them and that.

Horses were getting unhitched and patrons were getting the hell out, some on foot, as Cesar came around the corner and took in the carnage with disappointment.

"I guess I close up for the night," he said.

"Do that," York said, sliding the hot handgun into its home. "Then go down and wake up Perkins."

This was the one part of town where the undertaker's hearing was less than keen.

Cesar sighed and trundled off, swearing softly to himself in Spanish.

York looked down at the dead saddle tramps, who were staring into eternity with dumb expressions, tangled together like lovers, and felt a pang of regret. Not for killing them, or for their loss to the family of man.

No.

But he would rather have taken them into custody and seen what he could get out of them, before turning them over to a judge and, in the case of Johnson anyway, a hangman.

While he waited, he went around to the Morgan horse and checked the saddlebags. They were empty but for one thing: half-a-dozen empty pouches marked FIRST BANK OF TRINIDAD.

Bill Johnson tracked down and dead, but only two hundred to show for it.

And of all places to hide, of every place the robber might go, why double-back to Trinidad?

CHAPTER SIX

Caleb York knew that, no matter what the dime novels might have you believe, bank robberies in the West were not an everyday thing. If anything, they were rare. A bank was usually the most solidly built structure in town, and the redbrick First Bank of Trinidad was no exception.

Like most banks in Western communities, First was right on Main Street, in the center of town. Nighttime robberies almost never happened—blasting through reinforced walls was hard, noisy work. Robbers riding up in daylight, going in with guns out, and coming back with saddlebags full of loot often faced citizens—whose financial lifeblood the robbers had just drained—with guns ready to shoot, not to mention lawmen ready to do the same.

And in the day before yesterday's robbery, that very thing had happened—citizen Caleb York had shot and killed two of the thieves, and Sheriff Ben Wade had been in the thick of it, too. Only Wade had died, and the bandit with the greenback-stuffed saddlebags had made his escape.

The bank opened at nine A.M., but Caleb at eight-thirty knocked on the glass and was let in one of the double doors by clerk Herbert Upton, a weak-chinned, clean-shaven, bespectacled little man in a dark gray jacket, black tie, and black pants.

The single-room interior of the bank was modest in size but elaborate in appearance, fine wood, brass fittings, marble floor. All this implied wealth on the banker's part and suggested stability and permanence for his facility... though men with guns had recently challenged that notion. The three brass-barred cashier windows were plenty for Trinidad's needs, and the big rectangular iron safe against the back wall, by a map of the New Mexico territory, had a formidable heft.

Upton relocked the door and said in a mid-range reedy voice, "Congratulations, Sheriff. On getting that scalawag, I mean."

That sounded like York had brought in a kid who'd stolen laundry off a line. But what the scrawny clerk referred to, of course, was Bill Johnson.

"Thanks, Mr. Upton."

Though the morning had barely begun, everyone in town surely knew about Johnson's demise, since undertaker Perkins already had the corpse propped up in the funeral parlor window, with a sign that read KILLED BY OUR FINE SHERIFF. York had taken a look himself, and thought Johnson looked pretty fair, considering the extra nostril.

The president and owner of First, Thomas Carter, had no private office, just a big, impressive desk with a lot of fancy scrollwork on its edges, a barge that had dropped anchor behind a low wooden railing with a gate. Carter had been seated, going over a ledger, when York came in, but was on his feet now, though still at the desk. He issued a business-like smile and motioned for York to join him.

The large-framed banker's black, narrow-lapel cutaway coat revealed a gold-and-black embroidered vest with a gold watch chain; his trousers were black as well, though bearing a bold white vertical stripe. His collar was high and his bow tie was black. Like his lobby, he looked suitably impressive.

Before taking the customer's chair opposite the banker, York dropped his hat on the desk and also five empty First Bank canvas pouches with drawstrings, as deflated as dead balloons. Also before sitting, the sheriff withdrew from a pocket of his black trousers a wad of folded-in-half cash, a fairly thick bankroll consisting of various denomination bills.

"That's two hundred dollars," York said, "taken from Bill Johnson's pants shortly after he departed this life."

"Glad to have it," the banker said in that resonant baritone, though his single raised eyebrow was reflected in his tone. "I'll write you a receipt before you go."

The curling bills sat atop the closed ledger on the desk blotter like an accusation of incompetence—but whose?

"It's a start," York said, nodding at the money. "Not much of one. But a start."

The banker gestured magnanimously. "At least you set an example for others of this Johnson's kind."

"You've never been robbed before?"

"Not once in twelve years."

York shrugged. "Well, stagecoaches are easier prey. Railroads used to be, before Pinkerton started riding along armed to the teeth. Were all three of your clerk cages open during the robbery?"

A curt nod. "They were. And, as I've said, all of my clerks

have revolvers at the ready. But we had two customers in the bank at the time, and the robbers came in waving guns. I raised a hand toward my clerks, as if to say, 'The better part of valor is no resistance.' Money can sometimes be recovered. Human lives cannot."

"The two dead men in the undertaker's window yesterday, and the fresh one this morning, can testify to that. As for recovering the money, I'm hopeful."

Both eyebrows went up this time, and the banker leaned forward. "Are you? That's balm to my ears, sir. How do you arrive at this opinion?"

York leaned back in the hard chair, put his right ankle on his left knee, folded his arms. "An educated guess. The un–dearly departed William Johnson had several possibilities for escape. He was close to Las Vegas and the train, for example. And had he headed south, and made it over the border, he'd be livin' high on the Mexican hog right now—not serving as a warning in a window."

The banker was frowning in thought. "But he did neither of those things."

"That's right, Mr. Carter. He returned to Trinidad. From a standpoint of strategy, that has some appeal, chiefly how unexpected it was."

"I should think, sir."

York put both feet on the floor and sat forward. "But doing so carried considerable risk. Johnson may have figured he could get lost in that *barrio* with a pretty *señorita*. But considerin' that part of town is across from the sheriff's office, I would say his choice was ill-considered."

The banker cocked his head, narrowed his eyes. "Why ever would that villain come back to town, Mr. York?"

"Perhaps to meet up with an accomplice." Very quietly he said, "I'm considering the possibility that the robbery was an inside job."

Carter frowned. "An inside . . . that's *impossible,* sir. Simply out of the question. Everyone on my staff—all three clerks, and even the janitor—has been here since we opened."

"Eight years ago."

"That's right. You're not a native, Sheriff, so you don't know the history of this institution, or my role in it, but I would be happy to illuminate you."

"Don't think that's necessary," York said, leaning back, folding his arms again. "My guess is you rolled into town with a bankroll, maybe saved from working in big-city banks and learning the ropes for, say . . . five years? So you came to Trinidad and opened not a bank, but some other business. To establish yourself as a citizen, trustworthy and upright."

A little surprised, Carter said, "Yes, the mercantile store was originally mine. I moved here with my wife, rest her soul, from Albuquerque. I sold out to Harris when I had saved sufficient funds to back and open this bank. With so much ranching in the area, it was needed. . . . Ellis was getting all that business. One of my clerks . . . Mr. Upton, the gentleman who let you in the door? . . . was with me at the mercantile."

"What kind of money does Upton pull?"

The banker frowned, perhaps offended. "Aren't you wading into waters that are none of your concern, Sheriff? Shouldn't my people, shouldn't *any* good citizen, have a certain amount of privacy?"

"Your bank was robbed. Men died. How much, Mr. Carter?"

He harrumphed. "Well, I recently promoted Mr. Upton to chief cashier. Really, his position hasn't changed, but I felt he deserved a share of . . . prestige. For his years and his loyalty."

"You haven't answered my question, sir."

He kept his voice low, his manner confidential. "Of course, you must keep in mind that we don't work the normal sixty-hour week. It's around forty. Bankers' hours, as they say. So Mr. Upton's ten dollars a week is, I would say, generous."

York and the banker had differing definitions of the word "generous." But he did not press that.

Instead, York said, "These empty bank pouches that I found in Johnson's saddlebags. How much do they hold?"

Carter turned over a hand. "Well, obviously, such bags can accommodate various amounts, depending upon whether it's cash or coin, and what the denominations might be. There's no standard answer, Sheriff."

"What did they hold the day Johnson and his *amigos* knocked over this bank?"

The banker's tongue came out and caught his mustache, as if he were trying to taste it. "Five thousand dollars."

"Total?"

"Each."

York gave a slow whistle. "Five thousand dollars. Five bags. Was that the take, then? Twenty-five thousand dollars?"

He nodded. "They didn't bother with the cash drawers, or the coin. They wanted the money pouches."

"Why the hell did these bags have so much cash in them?"

With the patience of a father explaining something to a slow child, Carter said, "Trinidad's a ranching center, Sheriff. You know the kind of money that comes through those doors and into that safe. Periodically we send bags of cash to the Union Bank in Denver. A Wells Fargo run was scheduled for later this week."

"So those bags of money were just waiting here for Johnson and his boys."

The banker's eyes widened and quiet indignation came into his voice. "Sheriff York, what you're implying is irresponsible."

"Maybe. But I've been in this bank before, Mr. Carter. I had an account here I closed out last week, you'll recall, when I believed I'd be leaving."

"Yes. We can put that back in effect anytime you like, of course."

York waved that off. "That big safe back there—mighty impressive. But every time I came in here, I noticed it was standin' open. Isn't that awful risky?"

Now something like embarrassment was crawling up the high collars. "It had never proved so before. In *retrospect . . .*"

"Then why do it?"

"Sir, it's a common practice in Western banks. Folks of pioneer stock don't trust a safe with its door closed."

"That's funny. I'd think just the opposite."

The banker shook his head. "To the contrary. The depositors prefer a full view of their money stacked within, and the sight of that metal door, many inches thick. It provides the appearance of safety."

"*Appearance* is right."

Carter's voice grew cold. "Sheriff, your manner is beginning to grate upon me."

"You and the rest of the Citizens Committee didn't ask me to stay on because of my charm. Don't you also have bars of gold and silver in that safe?"

"We do. Those and the cash and coin in the cashier-window drawers were all that remained. Not enough to stay solvent. With my own infusion of funds, however, and what Mr. Zachary Gauge intends to deposit . . . well, let us just say we had a very narrow escape, sir."

York gestured toward the safe, whose door today was very much closed. "Why didn't they take those bars of precious metal?"

"Too heavy."

"Or too much trouble." York nodded toward the safe. "If they knew those bags of cash were sitting there in an open safe, the thieves could risk a daring daylight robbery. Knowing they could pull it off in probably a minute."

The banker shrugged. "I would say your time estimate, at least, is correct."

"Then do you understand why I suspect an inside job?"

The man's chin came up. "I do not."

York shook his head. "Your top clerk, your 'chief cashier,' makes ten dollars a week. You don't think twenty-five *thousand* presents a temptation? What do the other two clerks make?"

". . . Eight dollars a week."

"And the janitor?"

"Five."

"I want to speak to all of them. We can do it here or at my office."

Alarm widened the banker's eyes. "Oh, not at your office, Sheriff. People would talk."

"I kind of think people are already talking, Mr. Carter."

The banker shook his head firmly. "You're wrong, Sheriff. You may be a man of sharp instincts and shrewd insights, but you misjudge this town. In a few moments, our doors will open. You'll see no run on this bank. I dare say no one will take me up on my offer, either, of paying out twenty-five cents on the dollar for those who wish to close out their accounts."

Not after Zachary saved your bacon, York thought.

"But I do understand your need," Carter said, with strained patience, "to speak to my employees. The janitor is only here afternoons and evenings, so we will have to arrange that for another time. But you can talk to my clerks here at my desk. I'll fill in for them at their windows as needed."

York talked to the three clerks, individually.

Eldon Howe—his features regular, his build slender—was in his thirties, lived in a boardinghouse, and was dating the preacher's daughter. He liked working with numbers, enjoyed people, and said with a shy smile, "The money is good here—and it's indoors and clean."

Plump, pleasant Wilburn Glascock was in his twenties, and he and his wife had a new baby boy. His wife had inherited a little money, and they owned a small house in town. Glascock seemed happy with his lot in life, and called the bank president "a fine man and fair to work for. We all get an extra five dollars at Christmas."

Each man acknowledged having a revolver in his cash drawer, but said that Carter and Upton had signaled not to use the weapons. With two customers in the bank at the time of the robbery, both men found this a prudent reaction.

The bank's new chief cashier, Upton, sang a similar song.

"He's a fine man, our Mr. Carter." His eyes were dark blue and set so close together near a knob of a nose, the round lenses of the wire glasses nearly bumped. "Trinidad is lucky indeed to have such a conscientious guardian of its treasure."

This voluntary endorsement struck York as trying too hard, so he pressed the issue.

"You don't think some of the practices here at the bank are suspect?"

"*Suspect?* What do you mean . . . 'suspect'?"

"Bagging that money up days before it was to be transferred. Safe doors standing open, where all of that cash was just begging to be stolen."

The clerk was shaking his head. "Customers get nervous, if they can't see the insides of that safe, piled with cash."

"But it wasn't piled with cash. It was piled with *bags* of cash. Easily transported. No withdrawal could have been quicker or easier."

Sweat pearled the man's high forehead, and it wasn't at all warm in the bank. "Just what are you implying, Sheriff?"

York gave the man a lazy half-smile. "Am I implying something? Other than perhaps ill-advised procedure?"

Thin lips twitched a frown. "Leaving the safe doors open has been standard practice since we opened. In eight years, there's never been a problem."

"You've been here since the start, I understand. And you worked at the mercantile before that, also for Mr. Carter?"

The cashier was nodding. "I did. As I say, he's a fine man. He's always taken care of me."

"How so?"

Upton flicked a nervous smile. "Just . . . he pays well, and steady."

"Are you a married man, sir?"

The close-set eyes blinked away sweat. "No. Uh, what does that have to do with the price of eggs?"

"Well, I guess it would double the price, since you'd be buying for two."

". . . I'm engaged."

"Congratulations. Who's the lucky lady?"

"Pearl Kenner."

"Over at the Victory?"

"She used to work there. She quit two weeks ago."

York grinned, keeping it friendly. "Well, sounds like she's getting ready to set up housekeeping. Are you thinking of buying a place?"

Upton swallowed thickly. "Pearl will just be moving into my room at the boardinghouse, for now—why? Why is this *your* business, Sheriff? I thought you were questioning me about the robbery."

York answered that with his own question: "You didn't happen to know Bill Johnson, did you, Mr. Upton? I'd imagine he frequented the Victory now and again."

"Never met the man."

"But maybe you knew him by sight or reputation."

"No."

York shrugged. "You're bound to know some of the rough bunch that Harry Gauge brought in, to deputy for him and work his ranches . . . right? Between the bank and the Victory?"

Upton shifted uncomfortably in his boss's chair. "No, I didn't know him by name or reputation, either. And, yes, like a lot of working people in this town, I go to the Victory for a drink in the evenings, sometimes. But when I know it's going to be a night where those rowdy cowboys are on the prowl . . . you know, payday night? . . . I avoid that place like poison."

York gave him another friendly grin. "Well, Pearl's a nice gal. Everybody likes Pearl."

Upton frowned. "Do you mean something by that, Sheriff?"

"No. Good luck to you lovebirds."

Upton stared at York with open contempt. "Is that all, sir? I need to get back to my station."

The bank was open, but there were no customers at the moment.

"Sure. Go send your boss over."

Upton frowned and went over to his window, where Carter was filling in for him. The clerk pointed toward the seated York, and employer and employee spoke for a while, in hushed tones, longer than it would seem necessary for him merely to dispatch his boss to rejoin the sheriff.

Finally, Carter came over and sat heavily in his chair, looking across the desk at York with put-upon eyes. "You seem to have upset my chief cashier."

"Apparently doesn't take much. I *will* want to speak with your janitor."

"Understood. His name's Charley Morton." The banker sat forward, his expression earnest now. "Sir, do you really hold out hope for recovering our funds?"

"I do. I think that money is hidden somewhere in town or anyway near it. And I intend to investigate the friends and co-workers of the three dead bank robbers, to possibly get a line on where."

"I would think you would find *that* low-class breed," the banker said with a half-sneer, "more suitable for suspicion than my loyal staff."

"You would think," he said with a smile.

York didn't put his hat back on until he was outside. He was heading down the boardwalk toward his office, spurs singing, when he heard a familiar female voice call out to him, raised over approaching hoofbeats.

"Caleb!"

He glanced back as Willa—in a red-and-black plaid shirt, Levi's, and boots (as was often the case), her blond hair ponytailed with a red ribbon—pulled back on the reins and brought Daisy, her calico, to a sudden stop. She had obviously ridden here fast, faster than prudent, judging by the lathered-up nature of the poor animal.

She hopped down and tied the horse up at the nearest hitching post. He waited for her. She almost ran to him.

"I hear Bill Johnson's dead."

He nodded toward the funeral parlor. "You can see for yourself, if you like. Had breakfast yet?"

"Just coffee at the ranch. Buy me some and tell me all about it."

They went to the café and took a table by the window. The bacon and scrambled eggs were always good here and that's what they had.

"I want to hear all about it," she said, having more coffee. She took it black, which either was a sign of strength or wariness over the freshness of the cream.

He drank coffee, too, as he told her about last night at the Cantina de Toro Rojo, leaving in all the excitement but not detailing the carnage. That was a wise choice, because breakfast arrived halfway through the telling.

Her expression, as she bit at a strip of bacon and chewed, was a mixture of concern and excitement. He knew that she liked the part of him that stirred her love of adventure—she preferred *The Three Musketeers* to *Wuthering Heights*—but he also realized she feared for his life, having witnessed firsthand just how brutal and dangerous confrontations with outlaws could be.

"With this Johnson character dead," she said, "does that mean you'll be leaving?"

"No."

She smiled. Her eyes said, *Good,* but her mouth didn't bother. She just bit off more bacon.

"I want to stick," he said, "until this thing is resolved."

She frowned. "Resolved? How so? In what way?"

"The trail of the robber led right back to Trinidad. The trail of the money, too. Something's wrong here, Willa. Really wrong."

"What is?"

He didn't want to say anything about the bank, and its defensive president and his sweating chief clerk. For one thing, he wasn't sure exactly what he thought about Carter and his staff, though definitely Upton was worth looking at hard. For another, he didn't want those suspicions getting around town. Willa was no gossip, but Levi's or not, she was female.

"It's an itch that's developing," he told her. "Not to the scratchin' stage just yet."

"You talked to Mr. Carter today?"

"I did."

A smile flickered on pretty lips. "Did he . . . say anything about making you a better offer?"

"A better offer for what?"

The smile flickered out. "For staying. For staying on, after this is . . . resolved. Better money, matching Pinkerton or more. Providing you improved living quarters."

York shook his head. "No. Not a word. After our conversation, I'm not so sure Carter would want me around any longer than he feels he must."

"Oh? Why?"

He waved off her question. "Never mind that. Doesn't matter either way."

Now she was frowning. "What do you mean?"

"I mean, after I *do* resolve this mess, I'm still leaving." He patted her hand. "Honey, nothing's changed. But maybe if your father and your new friend Zachary Gauge go in business, you won't need to hang around here, either. San Diego's a real pretty place. Ocean's way bigger than the Purgatory River."

She was only half-finished with breakfast. But the way she pushed it away, and stormed out without another word, York had to wonder if she was all the way finished with him.

CHAPTER SEVEN

On horseback, Willa stopped burning about halfway home and was overcome by a sadness that she refused to allow to turn into tears. What had begun as a mental diatribe, about what an impossible man Caleb York was, turned into a sense of loss at the reality of not having that impossible man in her life on a daily basis, as he'd been for over six months.

Trying to make Caleb see that she could not leave the Bar-O as long as her father needed her wasn't the issue; she knew he got that. What he did not understand was how important the Bar-O and cattle ranching were to her. That they were as much a part of her life as any man could ever be. That if she were to marry and bear children, to him or to anyone else, the Bar-O was where she wanted that to happen.

Riding up to the ranch only made her feel that all the more keenly as she approached the familiar log arch with the chain-hung plaque with the big carved O under a bold line, replicating the Bar-O brand. In early-afternoon sun, the assorted buildings had a soft-edged glow worthy of memory, the twin corrals at right and left, the pair of barns, the grain crib, log-cabin bunkhouse, cookhouse with its hand pump and long wooden bench. The house itself had, like Topsy, grown from its humble beginnings until now it was an impressive, often added-to sprawl of log-and-stone.

Two horses stood at the hitch rail. One she recognized as foreman Whit Murphy's cattle pony, a pinto; the other she'd never seen, and she would have remembered this distinctive snowflake Appaloosa with its silver-mounted Mexican saddle. She tied up Daisy—who she'd ridden not nearly so hard on the ride home—next to the dark, light-spotted animal, with its thin mane and tail. The animal gave her that unsettling, near-human look the breed was known for—as if to ask, *Do you belong here?*—and she climbed the broad wooden steps to the awning-shaded porch. The cut-glass and carved-wood door opened suddenly, giving her a small start, and Whit exited, looking unhappy.

"Something wrong?" she asked the foreman.

Whit Murphy was a weathered, lanky cowboy with a dark, droopy mustache. Seeing Willa, he removed his Texas-style Stetson. She was well aware Whit was sweet on her, but he'd never done anything about it and she'd never encouraged it, either.

"Nothin' wrong," Whit said with a sigh that had a growl in it, "that me learnin' to keep my place wouldn't cure."

He was slipping past her and she stopped him with a hand on his arm.

"Whit—what *is* it?"

He nodded to the Appaloosa at the hitch rail below. "The man that critter belongs to is sellin' your papa a bill o' goods, far as I'm concerned."

Whit started to go again and this time she stopped him with a sharp word: "*Whit.*"

He was already at the bottom of the porch steps, but he halted and she came down again.

"Spill it," she said.

He shook his head, dark tendrils of hair stuck to his forehead. "The old feller asks me to stick around and sit in on a meetin' with this Zachary Gauge joker. I got work to do. Them new boys don't know up from down without me to tell 'em. But I say, sure, I mean, your pop's the boss. So I sit in."

"And?"

He scowled. "And when that snake-oil salesman starts in on Mr. Cullen, I just got to askin' questions. I mean, what does some Eastern dude know about ranchin', anyhow?"

She nodded toward the Appaloosa. "He's got himself a nice horse."

"Yeah, and a nice saddle, because he's the type that thinks money can buy anything. So I call him on some of what he's puttin' out there. But your papa acts like I'm bein' disrespectful or rude or some damn thing . . . excuse the language."

"I'll get over it, Whit."

He pointed toward the house with his Stetson. "You best go in there, Miss Cullen, before your papa makes a consarned fool of himself."

As the foreman rode off, a little harder than need be, Willa wasn't sure whether to be amused or concerned. She went quickly inside to see which was warranted.

Moving through the entry into the beam-ceilinged living room—where her father's rough-hewn carpentry mingled surprisingly well with her late mother's beautifully carved Spanish-style furniture—she found Papa and his guest seated in two Indian-blanket-covered, rough-wood chairs near the unlit stone fireplace at the far end of the room.

The ranch house had a lodge feel to it—hides on the floor, deer heads on the walls, with deer-hoof gun racks on either side of the fireplace, at left holding a Sharps rifle and at right a Winchester. Both weapons were functional, but the Sharps carried special significance—Papa had come West with not much more than a horse and that rifle. Buffalo hunting had built the grubstake from which Papa's first cattle herd came.

"Ah!" Papa said, rising. "Here's my daughter!"

He knew her footfall.

Zachary Gauge stood as well. He was again in black frock coat with fancy waistcoat and black silk tie. She couldn't decide whether his apparel reminded her more of a preacher or a gambler. But she appreciated the warmth of his smile as she approached.

She paused, the two men standing at the rough chairs, the backs of which were to her. "Has my father offered you anything to drink?"

Zachary waved that off. "Oh, that's kind, Miss Cullen, but not necessary."

She stood with her hands fig-leafed before her, a hostess in plaid shirt and jeans. "Nonsense. There's some coffee left from this morning. I'll heat it up. Might be strong enough to make your eyes water, at this point. But it should wet the whistle."

Her father said, "Please do that, Willa. It's the simple, civilized niceties that a blind old man can't offer properly. . . . Unless you'd like a glass of hard cider, Mr. Gauge?"

Zachary raised his palms in surrender. "Coffee will be just fine. Perhaps some cream and sugar?"

Her father asked for a cup, black, and she went off to fill the orders. She returned, set the cups on a silver tray on the small rustic table between the two big chairs, and—with her own cup of coffee—sat on the hearth facing the two men, but also between them.

This was a most conscious choice, as a chair Whit had obviously vacated was over by her father.

"It's very neighborly of you," she said to their guest, "dropping by to say hello like this."

A half-smile curled in the narrow oval of his face. Those cheekbones seemed borrowed from an Apache, and the wide-set dark eyes had an almost Oriental cast. And a better barber than their mayor had cut that hair and trimmed that mustache.

No question about it, she thought. *Zachary Gauge was a handsome devil.*

"This is not just a social call, Miss Cullen," he said, in his smooth second tenor. "We've paid our mutual respects already, at the Grange Hall. I'm here taking your father up on his offer to talk business."

Willa smiled, but tightly. "Well, let's not rush into things." She turned toward her father. "Have I missed anything, Father? You haven't sold Mr. Gauge my calico, have you? I'm fond of Daisy, and, anyway, our visitor already has a handsome horse."

Papa said, "We're still getting to know each other, Daughter. Let's stay hospitable."

She shifted her smiling but serious gaze to their guest. "Well, Mr. Gauge here seems to think the socializing is over and the business has begun. What business, exactly, is it we're discussing?"

"Miss Cullen," Zachary said, sitting forward, hands clasped between his knees, "you are right to be cautious. Everything today that we discuss is . . . preliminary. Exploratory."

"That's a relief. As I say, I'm fond of my calico."

He chuckled softly. "Your calico is quite removed from my evil designs."

"How wonderful to hear. What *are* your evil designs, now that you mention them?"

Her father frowned at her. "Daughter . . ."

But Zachary said, "As I said at the Grange, Miss Cullen, I'm cattle poor . . . at least for the moment. On the other hand, I have three times as much land as your father does."

"As my father and *I* do," she corrected gently.

"Forgive me. I am aware that you . . ." He seemed about to say "help your father," but instead said, ". . . are a key part of what makes the Bar-O tick."

"She surely is," Papa put in.

"But consider," Zachary said, leaning back and gesturing with a slender-fingered hand, one that she doubted had seen physical labor in some time if ever, "between us we could become a virtual cattle empire in this part of the world. Sir, you could be the next John Chisum. We would be second to none in the entire New Mexico territory."

"Us with all our cows," she said, "you with all that land. Land, that is, with no cows on it."

Another smile. They came easily to him. "That can be remedied with money. And I *have* money. What I don't have is experience in the cattle business, much less expertise. Now in business *period,* I have considerable experience and for that matter considerable expertise. I would pull my weight. I would add to the enterprise."

"What exactly are you suggesting?" she asked.

"I'm suggesting you consider a proposal to merge our holdings, much as industries back East merge into more powerful, bigger industries." Zachary looked toward the sightless man. "I'm not suggesting that you sell me a few cattle . . . a starter herd . . . no."

But Papa already knew that, and he said to her, "Zachary would like to use my know-how . . . *our* know-how . . . and connections in the cattle trade . . . to build a herd twice the size of what we now have."

"And that would only be the start," Zachary said.

"Partners," she said.

"Yes. Fifty-fifty. Really, I'll be contributing more, because I have more land and my funds will purchase enough cattle to, as your father said, double the size of your herd."

"Why so generous?" she asked.

He flipped a hand. "Because I am an infant in the cattle business. I want to partner with people who know what they're doing. Who are respected, knowledgeable cattle ranchers."

She mulled it for a few moments. Then she said, "This is something Papa and I will need to discuss. At length."

"Of course it is. But with your permission, I will start some paperwork. Is there a reliable lawyer in town?"

"Now, Mr. Gauge," Willa said, cocking her head, "aren't you jumping the gun a little?"

"We need to move quickly," Zachary said. "I know enough about the cattle business to understand that by spring we need to be a well-oiled machine. If we're to take our combined herd to market in the most fruitful way."

"I don't see any harm," Papa said.

Zachary, like any good salesman, knew enough to assume the sale. He got to his feet. "I understand there are two lawyers in Trinidad. Do you have a preference? Or should we go to Las Vegas or Albuquerque for counsel?"

"Arlen Curtis is my legal man," her father said.

"Then he's good enough for me. I'll have all the necessary documents for you to examine—deeds, land surveys, and so on."

Her father was on his feet, beaming at the man, as if he could see him. "We look forward to receiving them, sir."

Willa said, "I'll walk you out, Mr. Gauge."

She did that.

On the porch, with the door shut and her father well out of earshot, she said, "If you think I'm about to let you roll over us like a runaway stage—"

"I would be very foolish," he said, a black Stetson in hand, "to even dream of putting anything shady past you. Your father is a good man, and I think in his day, he may have been a great one."

"You're not wrong."

He gave her a smile with something puckish in it. "But I have no misconceptions about who runs this ranch, Miss Cullen." His smile softened into the mere friendly. "I don't suppose you'd allow me to call you 'Willa'?"

"Please do. I would rather call you 'Zachary' than 'Mr. Gauge,' as you yourself already suggested."

"I'm pleased to hear that."

"Don't be. I just don't like the name 'Gauge.' Good afternoon, Zachary."

And she went inside, leaving him to his Appaloosa.

Lem Rhomer was playing cards in the Silver Dollar Saloon in Las Vegas, New Mexico. In Las Vegas, with its population of four thousand, a man in search of gambling, drink, and trollops had half-a-dozen choices, and the Silver Dollar was the worst and roughest of these. Here was where you were the most likely to be cheated, served rotgut, or contract the French disease.

Last month the first two of these unfortunate results had been Lem's fate at the Silver Dollar. As for the French disease, the elder Rhomer boy—Lem was a ripe old forty—

did business with no loose women without the protection of a tight lambskin.

But the crooked dealer at the Dollar's poker table had taken Lem for a hundred dollars, and the rotgut proved so bad, he'd wound up puking in an alley and woke up there hours later rolled of what bankroll the dealer had left him, and with a blinding headache that lasted for three days.

Redheaded, wiry-bearded Lem was a big man, the biggest of the Rhomer boys, six foot one and with a muscular frame developed on their daddy's farm in Missouri. On his own and sometimes with his brothers, he'd worked a few cattle drives but mostly found better ways to make a living. Hiring out his gun and robbing people and places, mostly.

The dealer at the Dollar was small and bald and mild with babyish features and a pair of eyeglasses that had a barely noticeable pink tinge to them. His suit was tan and his shirt ruffled. Over the course of an evening, he always came out ahead.

Lem had never got wise—hell, the house always had the advantage, right?—but the middle Rhomer brother, Luke, had gone around to the Dollar to check up on things, after Lem's bad night there.

"He's usin' readers," Luke reported back to his older brother.

"Marked cards? I suspected as much, but I looked 'em over careful. Didn't see no marks or nicks."

Luke, like all the Rhomer boys, had their father's red hair—also his foul temper and cruel streak. "You can't see the markin' without special glasses. That's what them pink spectacles do. They show him patterns on the back of the cards that your eyes can't see."

"Cheatin' bastard! You think he's on his own, or is the house crooked?"

"Oh," Luke said, "it's the house. Roulette wheel's rigged, too. There's a toe brake under the table. Every damn game of chance in that hole has about as much chance to it as a two-headed coin in a toss."

Lem got himself in a tizzy. "I'll get even. I swear I'll get even. I'll rip them beady eyes out of his face and then see what good them glasses do him."

That made Luke grin. "Why not take the whole house down? That crooked dealer is just a cog. Why not rattle the whole damn wheel?"

Luke always did have ambition.

Lem said, "You gonna help?"

"Sure I'll help. We'll get all the brothers to help."

Of course, one brother couldn't take part—Vint, the second-to-the-oldest, who'd been Harry Gauge's deputy in Trinidad. Vint had been gunned down, and not by just anybody—Caleb York himself.

Vint had been one rough apple. It would take a Caleb York to take Vint Rhomer down. The Rhomer brothers were proud of that. Of course, one of these days they would have to blow Caleb York's brains out. But with the brothers scattered to the four winds, doing this and that, thieving around the Southwest alone and in pairs, it would take a regular family reunion to make getting even with Caleb York come true. If Vint by himself couldn't handle the legendary York, they would have to band together for it.

And it did sound like a good time.

Who'd have guessed that the Silver Dollar in Las Vegas would provide the spark? That the tiny revenge the Dollar was due would spark the bigger revenge that son of a bitch York had coming?

Anyway, with his brothers spread around the Dollar, playing crooked games, romancing the painted ladies,

Lem sat for a good hour gambling reckless with the cheat in the cheaters, letting the little coyote think he was fleecing this lamb for a second time. If the S.O.B. even recognized Lem from a few months before.

It was very damn quiet. Middle of the afternoon. Lem, Sam, Luke, Les, Eph, were half the customers. Real slow time at the Dollar. Three girls. One bartender. A manager back in his office. A roulette table, a craps table, neither with suckers right now. Two other players at the poker table.

While the little dealer in the pink eyeglasses was shuffling the cards, a cowboy with a lot of mustache said, like he was just making conversation, "You're Lem Rhomer, ain't you?"

"Who's askin'?"

"Just a feller from Trinidad doin' some business in the big city."

The little man in the pink shades started dealing stud, five-card. Lem held up a hand to stop him.

"Gimme a minute, friend," Lem said to the cheating bastard.

"Glad to oblige," the cheating bastard said.

The cowboy full of mustache said, "I knew your brother. Fine feller, Vint. Too bad that York buzzard took him out like that."

"Yeah," Lem said. "Goddamn shame. I loved him like a brother. Uh . . . of course he *was* one."

"You know," the cowboy said, checking the hole card that was as far as the deal had got before Lem put it on hold, "that York was supposed to leave Trinidad. But then the bank got stuck up and the sheriff what took York's place got hisself killed."

"That right."

"And York's gonna hang awhile, around Trinidad, till that's all sorted out. He's already killed the three robbers."

"Then why's he sticking?"

The cowboy shrugged. "Lookin' for the money, I guess. Funny thing, though."

"What's funny about it?"

"I know a guy who would pay *real* money to get rid of that man."

"What man?"

"What man you think? Caleb York."

"Are you just talkin' through that hat?"

"No. I'm prepared to do business."

". . . You know where the Plaza Hotel is?"

"I do."

"After this hand, cash out, and meet me over there. In half a hour, say."

"I can do that. Way things is going, I won't have to cash out. I'll lose the rest of these chips."

That proved to be the case. The little cowboy tipped his hat and left. The other player did the same, after cashing out for less than five dollars.

The dealer said, "You wanna play two-handed, mister? Some folks don't cotton to that."

"I like two-handed fine. But give me them glasses first."

"What?"

"My eyes is hurtin' me. Must be the smoke. Let me borrow them glasses of yours."

The derringer came out quick, but Lem's .45 was already drawn under the table. He blew the dealer's guts out. The smell of gunpowder and bowels vacating at dying filled the room along with the screams of trollops.

The bartender came up with a shotgun and brother Luke shot him in the face, decorating the mirror behind the dead man a dripping scarlet. The manager, a well-fed man in a fancy red vest, didn't die, not right away, because Eph's gun was all of a sudden in his neck. Eph and Les accompanied him into the office and after two minutes or so, and a gunshot, the redheaded brothers came out with a bag of money from the Dollar safe.

Lem had already emptied the dealer's money box. The soiled doves in spangles and the men running the other games were hiding under tables, as were the couple of patrons, when the Rhomer brothers went out into the sunshine, two thousand and five hundred and fifty six dollars and fifty cents the better.

They got on their horses and rode across town to the hotel, where Lem would give them the good news about Caleb York and how they were going to get both revenge and more money out of it.

Much better than Lem's previous visit to the Dollar.

CHAPTER EIGHT

Caleb York peered over the batwing doors of the Victory Saloon and saw what he hoped he would: a quiet night.

Weeknights often were less than hopping at Trinidad's only, if imposing watering hole. Payday weekends were wild—many of the merchants boarded up their windows—and really any weekend could be a ripsnorter. But right now the Victory was in the midst of a lull.

He pushed through the swinging doors and glanced around. The Victory always looked big, but seemed mammoth when it wasn't doing much business, its ornate tin ceiling like an endless sky lit by the suns of gas-lamp chandeliers, its fancy gold-and-black brocade wallpaper everywhere. The long, highly polished oak bar over at left seemed to go on forever, mirrors and bottles of bourbon and rye, towels dangling for fastidious types to wipe foam from their mustaches, a shiny brass foot rail with frequent spittoons. Behind the bar, on a busy night, as many as five bow-tied, white-shirted bartenders might be at work, serving the thirsty horde. Tonight, only one, and the customers were mostly townsfolk.

The casino section of the place was a ghost town, no one working the various stations, from roulette to wheel-of-fortune. One faro table, one poker table, were all that were going. Two bored-looking satin-clad darlings sat at a table challenging the established mores by smoking cheroots as one helped the other play solitaire. At the far end of the big room, the little stage was empty and so was the bench at the upright piano.

York went to the bar, which he had to himself, like one religious man at an immense altar. The bartender, whose name was Hub Wainwright—a big man with thinning brown hair and a round face and the kind of shoulders that said he could do his own bouncing—knew to give the sheriff a beer. Hub also knew not to refuse the sheriff's dime.

York sipped the warm beer. "Slow night."

"I heard you was a detective."

York smiled, rather liking Hub's dry sense of humor. "Is the boss lady in?"

"Look to your right."

Rita Filley, who had inherited the Victory from her murdered sister, might have been Lola's ghost. Though he would never ask a female such a thing, he felt sure the dark-haired Rita, whose slender, full-breasted shape so recalled Lola's, had assumed not only her late sister's business but her wardrobe as well.

He would swear he had seen Lola in that same blue-and-gray satin gown, its black lace cupping the sister's bosom lovingly, the dress parted in front like curtains on a stage to show off fishnet silk stockings and laced-up high-heel shoes.

This young woman had near the same oval face with big brown eyes, turned-up nose, and full, red-rouged lips.

There were differences, though—Lola's beauty mark near that sensual mouth had been real, and those big eyes weren't as widely set. Rita here was new to the saloon trade and hadn't lost all the softness in her pretty face. Yet.

"Good evening, Sheriff," she said, depositing herself before him. Her voice was higher than Lola's had been, though some of the sister's throaty purr lurked in there, too. "You might as well take that badge off—there's no trouble here tonight."

"I'll leave it on just the same," he said, though he'd already removed his hat in her presence. "You never can tell."

She gave him half a smile, though the dark eyes were completely amused. "You're a poker player, aren't you?"

"I am."

She jerked a thumb over her shoulder. "There's a chair open. Several of Trinidad's most distinguished bad card players are seated there. Could be a golden opportunity."

"I'd rather seize a different opportunity, Miss Filley."

"Oh?"

He nodded. "I'd like to finally have a chat with you. We've never really talked."

"I had the feeling you didn't see the need—since you were leaving town and all."

With a shrug, he said, "Well, I'm still here. Why don't we take a table?"

All of the tables, opposite the bar, were empty.

"I think we can squeeze in," she said, and looped her arm in his.

He walked her over. Pulled a chair out for her.

She sat and looked up at him with an expression that already conveyed some fondness, or pretended to. "You're a rarity in these parts, Sheriff."

"My name is Caleb."

She gestured to the chair next to her. "Sit down, Caleb. And I'll tell you why you're such a rare breed."

He sat.

She did: "You take your hat off in a lady's presence. You pull out a lady's chair. You call me 'Miss Filley.' If you're trying to get on my good side, you're doing a very nice job of it."

He sipped the warm beer, then said, "I think I just stumbled."

"Did you?"

"I should have asked if you wanted something to drink."

"Sheriff . . . Caleb? I own the place. And men don't buy me drinks. They buy my girls drinks. Is that why you're here?"

"Pardon?"

"To talk to me about my girls? Sheriff . . . and right now I am speaking to the sheriff . . . I want you to know that I intend to make some changes here. Some of these girls are going to be going."

"Going where?"

She batted the air with a lacy-gloved hand. "Anywhere but here. I assume you were planning to get around to making me divest myself of my fallen angels, so I'll ask for your patience. Give me a few months."

"A few months for what?"

She gestured with the other lace-gloved hand. "To make this place more respectable. I have no need and no interest in running a house of ill repute. The more respectable drinking and gambling emporiums have girls who dance with the male customers, who let those customers buy them drinks, and encourage gambling. Sing, dance, talk, flirt."

They paused in conversation as bartender Hub brought her a drink. "Your Mule Skinner, madam."

Whiskey and blackberry liqueur.

"Thank you, Mr. Wainwright," she said.

He disappeared.

York asked her, "What are you going to do with all those rooms upstairs?"

She sipped her drink, shrugged with her eyebrows. "I'm going to live in them, after some fix-up and new furnishings. I'll have an office up there, too. Little rathole downstairs doesn't suit me. I know you have a reputation as a . . . a . . ."

"Prude? Prig?"

She frowned, shook her head. "No. I know that's not the case. My sister wrote me letters. She wrote me one shortly before she passed that was very . . . *complimentary* about you. Reading between the lines, I gathered . . . well, that's neither here nor there."

He shifted in his chair. "Isn't it? I was sheriff here for six months. I didn't try to shoo the soiled doves from their cages during that time. Why do you assume I would now?"

The dark eyes widened. "Because, as you say, you're still here. Before, you were just holding down the office till the town found somebody to fill it, and when they didn't, you went out and got poor Ben Wade. Now that you're *staying*—"

"You've been misinformed. I'm only staying until this bank robbery is cleared up."

Her smile seemed faintly mocking. "You killed the robbers and yet here you sit. No, I have a feeling you may be here awhile longer. Maybe a lot longer. I'm aware of Miss Willa Cullen, and how you two . . . well. Again. Neither here nor there."

He frowned at her. "Your sister wrote you about that, did she?"

"She did. But I have eyes. I've only been here two weeks, but I have eyes." She drew in breath and let it out, then sat forward slightly. "Listen, Sheriff . . . Caleb . . . I want to thank you. You deserve my thanks."

"Why is that?"

She waved a hand around her. "You allowed the Victory to stay open until everything was settled and I was able to move to Trinidad. To *decide* to move to Trinidad, I should say."

"You might have just sold the place."

"The legalities took a while. But I liked having this opportunity. My sister fared well here."

"Right up to when she was killed."

That blunt remark didn't faze her. "Very gallant of you, to try to dissuade me from this life. But as I think, I *hope,* I've made clear—the Victory will be more respectable under my sway. Lola had a partner in that *other* sheriff, the crooked one—Harry Gauge? She was no brothel madam. He *made* her one."

"May I ask what you were doing, Miss Filley, before you took on your sister's business?"

"It's Rita. By 'doing,' you mean—for a living? I've been one of those dance-hall girls we were discussing— the ones who make a man feel good *without* going upstairs. I'm not new to this kind of place."

He was looking her over, realizing that behind the lip rouge and dance-hall gown, someone young was on view. "How old are you, anyway?"

"You would ask a female such a question? So much for gallantry, Caleb. I am twenty-four."

Still sizing her up, he said, "What kind of name is Filley? If you don't mind my asking."

"It's Irish. But my mother was Mexican. I grew up this side of the border. My papa was a blacksmith—not a family business either Sis or I could go into. When he died, the blacksmith shop went to Lola and she sold it. Came here and opened this palace."

He nodded. "It is something of a palace. I think you could do well here, even without the doves. Probably even better. Times are changing."

"I've noticed."

"This town will grow."

"Is that why you're staying on, Caleb?"

"I'm not staying on. Told you that."

"We'll see. So. Do we know each other better now?"

"I think so. But we do have more to discuss, if you're of a mind."

"Please."

"What's your relationship with Zachary Gauge?"

She frowned, shook her head. "I have no . . . relationship with him. Business or otherwise. I've never met the man. I understand he's in town. Like you, I'm sure he'll get around to looking me up and sitting me down."

York's gaze turned narrow-eyed. "But I gather he signed his interest in this saloon over to you."

"He did."

"And you never *met* him?"

An elaborate shrug. "It was done through attorneys. All by wire and mail. He was in New York. I was in Houston. It took a while, but he signed everything over to me."

"For nothing?"

"For one dollar." She smiled. "That was something the lawyers insisted on."

"Why would he do that?"

The big eyes grew wide again. "Maybe you should sit him down and ask him?"

But York pressed: "Zachary didn't say? I know you never met him, Rita, but in a letter . . . or through his attorney . . . ?"

She gestured with open hands. "Caleb, I gathered he didn't want to have any part of this place. Of a business like this. My feeling is he wanted to put a distance between himself and that black-sheep cousin of his. From what I hear, along those lines, he made a good impression at the Grange the other night."

"He did."

She shrugged, smiled. "Well, that explains it. You can't be an upstanding citizen and run a saloon with an upstairs brothel. The womenfolk and the preachers just won't have it."

York thought about that. It made sense.

He hadn't yet got to the real reason, or anyway the main one, that he'd come tonight. Much of his afternoon had gone to sending out another raft of telegrams, this time asking the sheriffs all around the territory to let him know if any of Harry Gauge's old gang showed up in their vicinity.

Then he said, "I like you, Rita."

"This is so sudden."

He flashed a grin. "What I mean to say is . . . you impress me as someone I might be able to trust."

Her eyebrows went up. "I've heard more ringing endorsements." Then down. "What do you have in mind, Caleb?"

He leaned in. "You're new here, but your people on staff aren't—the bartenders, the girls, your gambling crew. . . . I need to know when any of Harry Gauge's bunch come in here."

She mulled it momentarily, then shrugged and said, "I guess I could do that. But, as you say, I wouldn't recognize them."

"Well, you might. Your sister's partner brought in outlaws and gunhands and set them up as cowboys and deputies, when it's easy to see they aren't. Some have flown the coop. But others are still around."

She was nodding. "All right. I'll try. See what I can do."

He gave her a tight smile. "Good. The three bank robbers, who have lately been appearing in the undertaker's window . . ."

"I saw their show. They stink."

That loosened up his smile. "Be that as it may, they were all former Gauge cronies. And if the thieves had *accomplices* . . ."

"It would be former Gauge men." Nodding again. "I follow."

He held her eyes. "Somebody has the money that Bill Johnson and his buddies hauled out of First Bank. I want to find it. I want to give it back to the town."

She had a different kind of smile going now. Might call it wistful. "You are a gent, Caleb York. No wonder they write stories about you." She raised her glass. "To Caleb York. First legend I ever shared a table with."

"Don't be so impressed," he said.

"Why not?"

"Don't you know what the word 'legend' means? It's a myth. Something widely believed in, but just not true."

Tulley had slept most of the day.

The sheriff had put him on night patrol, and that meant a lot of prowling around, checking doors and alleys. The work was nerve-racking at times but mostly dull. During the day, Tulley slept on a cot in one of the cells at the rear of the office, because Clem over at the livery was put out with him for quitting and wouldn't let him sleep in his usual corner.

His stint on night patrol started at sundown and he was to keep it up for an hour after the Victory closed. Right now the saloon was open—it was going on eleven P.M. The place had no set closing time, but this time of week, business would be slow. By one A.M., they'd likely close the shutters over them batwing doors and lock up all around. So by two A.M. or so, he could hit the cot in that cell again.

Till tonight, Tulley had been walking on a cloud. A deputy! With his own badge! His own scattergun! And, thanks to Caleb York, the Citizens Committee had agreed to pay him forty dollars a month. The last time he made forty dollars was that silver strike that petered out the second week.

But walking up and down this sandy street made him thirsty. He was dragging. He looked almost longingly at the boardwalk he had so often crawled under to sleep, and sleep it off. It was cool under there in the warm times, and warm in the cool ones. He reckoned a man never had a more cozy resting spot betwixt womb and grave.

And he had traded that snug nest, and the companionship of a good bottle, for a *jail cell*?

Of course, Caleb York said he'd find Tulley something better. Just give him time. But time was something Caleb York didn't have—Tulley knew the sheriff was only here for now. That when the robbery matter was wrapped up in a bow, Caleb York and his reputation would get on the stage, and then where would Tulley be?

Would the next sheriff keep him on?

Not likely. Not dang likely. Not damn likely.

His gut was twitching with the want of God's sweet

nectar. His throat ain't felt this parched since the mule before Daisy up and died on him in the desert. He sat on the boardwalk steps in front of the hardware store and thought about his lot in life, the scattergun across his lap. He might have cried some.

Then got to his feet, shook the feeling off, told that damn thirst to crawl back in its hole, and Deputy Jonathan Tulley strode with pride down the street. Very much on patrol. And he was fine, just fine until he stepped into the pool of light spilling from the Victory.

He crept up to the batwing doors and peeked over, and in.

Hell's bells but it was dead in there. Hardly a soul. Some men playing poker and that was about all she wrote. The fancy girls was at a table smoking little cee-gars, and looking glum like flowers nobody wanted to pluck. One gal, the beautiful one that ran the place, was at the bar talking to Hub about something. Damn, she was fine to look at, spitting image of her dead sister, only younger and smoother of face.

But that only made Tulley sad again. When had he last been with a woman? Ten year? Twenty year? Twenty, since one he didn't pay. Ten, since he could afford paying. The thirst was back, raging like a fire in his belly that needed dousing right damn now.

He licked the driest lips in creation and pushed through them doors. He staggered like the drunk he hadn't been in ages over to the bar and he stood right next to Miss Rita.

He said, "Deputy Tulley. Makin' my nightly rounds, ma'am. Could ye stand me to a short one?"

She smiled on half her face, making one pretty dimple. "Do you deputies drink on the job?"

"Now and then we does. When the night calls for it."

"Sure about that, Deputy?"

She smiled wickedly and nodded over her shoulder.

At the poker table, a man in black with his back to Tulley was turning his way.

Sheriff Caleb York.

"Evening, Sheriff," Tulley said, too loud, grinning like a damn hyena. *"Just makin' my rounds!"*

Caleb York shrugged and returned to his game, as if he were saying, *Your choice, Deputy. Up to you.*

Tulley grinned at the boss lady. "Ma'am, what I mean to request is . . . have you any saspirilly?"

She did have, and Tulley drank the sarsaparilla down. The stuff had a patent-medicine taste with some licorice and vanilla mixed in. He didn't mind it none.

When he was finished, Tulley said, very loud, *"Well, that was the best dang saspirilly I had me in some time!"*

Caleb York, at the poker table, made a noise that Tulley thought might be a grunt or maybe a laugh.

Anyway, Tulley went on back out into the street, to continue his night rounds. While he was there, he checked the alley behind the Victory and, between some garbage barrels, he found a dead man.

On his side, kind of sprawled there, the little weak-chinned character had glasses on that was sitting crooked on his face, his eyes open but blank as a dolly's, his expression froze in something like surprise or pain or maybe both. Tulley didn't move the poor feller, but not being at all squeamish got down close to see that the belly of the nice gray vest under a gray jacket was blood-soaked.

But dried. Going black and crusty.

A scorched bullet hole, in the middle of all that dark red.

The deputy couldn't place him at first. It was dark back here, which didn't make it no easier. So the deputy flicked a kitchen match with a thumbnail and lit up the contorted face.

"Well, I'll be danged," Tulley said to no one who could hear.

It was that clerk from the bank.

That Herbert Upton.

Tulley ran and got the sheriff. After all, he knew right where he was.

CHAPTER NINE

Caleb York threw in his cards—all he had was a measly pair of deuces, anyway—but did take the time to collect his cash and coin before following his steamed-up deputy out of the Victory.

In the cool evening air, Tulley led York behind the building to the sideways figure on the ground between two garbage barrels, where the sheriff knelt and had a look. Tulley got a kitchen match going, sending flickery orange over the crumpled body.

"Fetch Doc Miller," York said, still crouched there looking at the corpse.

The doctor's living quarters were behind his simple waiting room and surgery on the second floor of the three-story bank building.

"Doc might be sleepin'," Tulley said, waving out the match.

"Wake him. Knock hard and keep knocking."

The deputy nodded and started off.

"Tulley!"

"Yes, Sheriff?"

"Tell Doc what you found. Tell him *who* you found.

And he can leave his medical bag behind. He already lost this patient."

"Yes, Sheriff."

"And, Tulley! Have Doc haul over one of those wicker baskets for bodies. He'll need your help with it."

Tulley nodded and ran off, fast as his bandy legs would let him, holding his scattergun high in one hand like a one-man Indian raiding party. If he dropped the thing, more than just Doc Miller would wake up. Whole damn town, maybe.

While he waited for the physician, York made his own diagnosis. Upton had been shot close-up—the powder burns told that tale. That meant the clerk got it from somebody he knew, probably somebody he trusted. The blood on the entry wound, blackened and crusted, meant the killing hadn't just happened. The larger wound in back, ragged and bloodier, was similarly black and clotted.

Some hours had passed since the trigger on a gun stuck in Upton's belly had been pulled. Maybe the doc could hazard a guess how many. But York doubted the crime had occurred here in this alley. On a busy night at the Victory, a shot might have got lost in honky-tonk piano and gambling din. On a quiet night like this one, the report of a weapon would have cut right through, and made itself known.

The lidless wicker coffin, bearing a sheet, arrived with Doc Miller—looking disheveled in a rumpled brown suit and no tie—at a handle on one side and Tulley on the other. York made room for them to set the basket down near the body.

The heavyset little physician, his white hair sleep askew, got right down there and had a look at the deceased; Tulley lit yet another kitchen match. The doctor glanced up at

York, catching some of the flame's orange. "I don't think you need a medical opinion on this one, Caleb."

"Oh but I do. I think he was moved. Shot somewhere else. Dumped here. What's *your* expert opinion?"

Having to work at it a little, the doc got back on his feet. "He was moved, all right. No blood in his face. Starting to settle."

York gestured to the dry ground at the victim's back. "And where's the blood that came out of him? If this happened here, that patch would be drenched with it."

The doc nodded. "Mr. Upton got shot and bled out. But not here." He shook his head, his expression glum— as much tragedy as this doctor had seen, Miller was still the kind of man who felt it. "Friend Upton died hard. He didn't pass out, either. Look at that expression."

York nodded, hands on his haunches. "All the pain in the world caught up with him. How long dead, you think?"

The stubby physician shrugged. "Somewhere between two and six hours."

"How d'you come up with that, Doc?"

"Rigor mortis hasn't set in yet. That's how long it takes—two to six hours. And in a few more hours, we can prove he was moved by where the blood settles."

"How so?"

The medical man gestured vaguely. "Way he was shot, right in the guts, a man doesn't land on his side, but on his backside. *That's* where the blood would gather. But if he was moved while the blood was still settling, we'll before long see the bruising look of it, on the side he's resting on."

York narrowed his eyes at Miller. "Then let's not wake up the undertaker just yet. Let's haul Mr. Upton to your surgery . . . place him on his side, just like that, in the wicker basket . . . and then ease him onto your table the same way. And see how your theory holds."

The doc found that a good enough plan.

Taking all this in, Tulley said, "I don't know doodlely-do about blood settlin', but I can just about gar-on-tee that this here bank clerk weren't killed in this alley. Or anywheres else outdoors in this town."

Genuinely interested, the doctor asked, "Why do you say that, Tulley?"

A many-hued grin blossomed in the bearded face. "Comes to gunfire, ol' undertaker Perkins has the devil's own hearin'. Betcha he sleeps in that there top hat and frock coat, so's he can git hisself to the scene of dyin' in a hell of a hurry."

Tulley was, of course, half-joking, but it got York to thinking.

He did some of it out loud: "Our undertaker friend is just a few doors down. And folks live in the spaces above these shops, all along here. *Somebody* would have heard the gunshot, if Upton got it anywhere around here."

"Even indoors," the doctor said, nodding. "Walls aren't exactly thick in these flimsy structures."

York frowned. "You think people maybe heard it, and decided to mind their own business?"

"In Trinidad?" The doc snorted a laugh. "The occasional shooting's the best entertainment this town can boast. Beats a musical recital at the Grange, don't you think? Anyway, did *you* hear a shot tonight?"

"No," York said.

"Me neither," Tulley said, "and I was out here walkin' patrol. How about you, Doc?"

"I heard no shot, but much of the evening I was out at the Watkins farm, lancing a boil on the middle boy's behind." The doc winced in thought, scratching his head. "Of course, I guess I wouldn't have heard it even if I'd been in."

"Why so?" York asked.

Miller shrugged. "Well, I live in the bank building, after all. Those walls are triple-thick. Reinforced."

"So they are," York said, looking in that direction. "So they are."

The next morning, Caleb York again knocked on the wood by the glass of one of First Bank's double doors a good half hour before those portals were to open for business. This time, however, he was not let in by Herbert Upton, who was at the funeral parlor at the moment, Doc Miller having turned him over to undertaker Perkins after the doctor and York witnessed the blue bruised effect of blood settling along the dead man's side.

On his third knock, York saw the bank janitor, Charley Morton—tall, thin, in his fifties, two white eyebrows the only hair on his head—come shambling over to see who was making such a racket. A friendly, googly-eyed skeleton of a man, Charley—in a work shirt a little too big and canvas trousers a little too short—bared his big yellow teeth in a smile, recognizing the sheriff.

Charley was the kind of guy who smiled whenever he recognized somebody.

"We ain't open, Sheriff," Charley said through the glass, grinning as if he'd just delivered good news.

"I know, Charley. Official business. Let me in."

Charley nodded and did so, locking the door behind them.

"You want to talk to me?" Charley said, with several nods that answered his own question.

The two men faced each other just inside the doors.

"Yes," York said, "we haven't had a chance to chat yet, have we, Charley? About the robbery?"

He shook his head, frowning. "That was a bad thing. I weren't here for that."

"I know, but I'm talking to all the bank employees about it. But right now I need to talk to Mr. Carter."

Carter was seated over at his desk, looking up from his ever-present ledger, clearly wondering why the sheriff had come around again, his frown landing just this side of irritated.

The janitor pointed. "Mr. Carter is seated over at his desk."

Charley's Adam's apple was prominent and moved up and down when he spoke.

"Yes, I can see that, Charley," York said pleasantly. "Say, you aren't usually here in the mornings, are you?"

"No, sir. I work in the afternoons and into the evening. When they's no customers around."

"Did you work yesterday evening?"

"No, sir. They's a church meeting Mr. Carter lets me off so's I can attend. Every Wednesday night, it is."

"That's kind of him."

"He is a God-fearing man, Mr. Carter is. He's over at his desk, Sheriff."

"Yes, Charley. Are you going to be around for a while?"

"Gotta finish up some cleaning back of the cashier cages, then I can go. We could talk then, iffen you like."

York patted him on a bony shoulder. "Maybe I could buy you a cup of coffee at the café, Charley."

The janitor smiled, eyes lighting up. "Or maybe a drink at the Victory? Beer maybe? People say I do some of my best talkin' after a beer at the Victory."

"Little early for that."

"Well, they's open!"

"I guess they are. You finish up and then wait till I've spoken to Mr. Carter, okay? And we'll have a beer at the Victory. A beer for breakfast."

"I already et my breakfast, Sheriff. But I can have a beer while you take sustenance."

"Great, Charley. Don't forget."

Charley grinned and shook his head. "I surely won't. Anyway, I got to get back to my mop and bucket."

The janitor ambled off. York wished everyone could be as happy with their lot in life as Charley. He wished he could.

The big, well-dressed banker was behind his desk but on his feet, waiting for York, who walked to the waiting visitor's chair. The two men shook hands and exchanged perfunctory smiles, then took their seats. York set his hat on the banker's desk.

"My apologies, Sheriff," Carter said with a flip of the hand. "I meant to send Charley around to talk to you, as you requested. It just slipped my mind. Fortunately, he happens to be here now."

"Rarely works mornings, I understand."

"Right. But he had some cleaning to tend to. Of course, I don't know how much you can hope to get out of Charley. He's rather a simple soul, as I'm sure you know."

"Well, out of the mouth of babes."

Carter twitched a smile at the biblical homily, then asked, "Is there, uh, anything else I can do for you, Sheriff? Is there any progress to report on your inquiry into the missing funds?"

"No progress, sir. I'm here on something unrelated. Something very sad. For this institution, even tragic."

Carter sat forward. "What is it, man?"

"Your clerk . . . your recently promoted chief cashier . . .

was found shot to death, last night. In the alley behind the Victory Saloon."

"Oh, my God, no." Carter sighed heavily, shook his head, then alert eyes flew to York. "What were the circumstances? Robbery?"

"Possibly. When Doctor Miller finished up his postmortem examination, I went through Mr. Upton's clothing. He had no money on him. Did he carry a watch and chain?"

The banker nodded. "He did. He was rather proud of that, actually. Gold. And a Swiss watch, inscribed by his father on the occasion of Herbert's twenty-first birthday."

"Well, watch and chain weren't on him. I haven't had a chance to check his lodgings yet."

Carter was shaking his head again, staring past York into nothing. "The Victory. I warned Herbert many times about that den of iniquity. He was seeing one of the girls there, you know."

"Right. Pearl Kenner. They were engaged, I understand."

A bitter laugh rumbled out of him. "That was Mr. Upton's belief, but I fear . . . I don't mean to speak out of turn. . . ."

"Please."

He raised an eyebrow and lowered his voice. "Rumor has it that this Pearl still works at the Victory. That while she told Herbert that she had quit—they were of late living together at his rooming house, in sin, you know—she continued working afternoons, when he was otherwise engaged here at the bank. Making a fool of him." A deep sigh. "And I'm afraid . . . I should leave it there."

"Please, go on."

Another sigh seemed to signal a decision to hold nothing back. "I'm afraid that I only encouraged this foolish adventure by giving Herbert a raise and that promotion. But he was a good man, a reliable man, and deserved as much. I'll be lost here, until I can find a suitable replacement."

Wouldn't that make a fine eulogy at the services, York thought.

The banker put a hand over his face and breathed hard. His other hand dug out a handkerchief and he touched it to his eyes.

"Forgive me," he said, choking up a little. "Herbert was . . . well, he was like a brother to me. Or rather . . . a son. My wife, rest her soul, and I, we never had any children, and I'm afraid I grew rather too fond of the young man over the years. He had a lovely manner."

"I didn't know him that well," York said. "Actually, I wonder if he wasn't less of a friend to this bank than you might think."

The handkerchief came away from eyes that looked pretty dry to York. "What is it you mean? Are you implying something . . . untoward, Sheriff?"

York didn't mince words: "I think Mr. Upton may have been the inside man on the bank robbery."

Carter's eyes showed plenty of white now. "*What?* Why, that's patently ridiculous. That's *absurd,* man!"

York shrugged. "Someone had to tell the robbers about that bagged-up money you were preparing to ship to Wells Fargo. Those boys knew just what to ask for, and just when to make their armed withdrawal. Your clerk was armed, too, but did nothing about the robbery, while it was under way."

Carter was puffing up with indignation. "Well, that was at *my* direction!"

"Perhaps. But as your highest-ranking clerk, Upton was in a position to either use his weapon, which he did not, or to discourage the other clerks from using theirs, which he did."

The banker was shaking his head so much, so hard, the air was stirring. "Sheriff, this doesn't sound like Herbert Upton *at all*. He was levelheaded, and this bank . . . and having a prominent position here . . . meant the world to him."

York turned a palm up. "But you said it yourself, Mr. Carter. He was on an adventure of love with a trained courtesan. Mr. Upton did not strike me as a Romeo or a Casanova. He was a rather homely man . . . meaning the deceased no disrespect. He might prove easy prey for a vampire female."

Carter was still shaking his head, but more slowly, as if York's words held that much weight. "If Herbert was one of them, as you say . . . and I find that preposterous . . . why did he wind up as . . . as he did?"

"I think the robbers, or another accomplice of theirs, considered Mr. Upton a loose end . . . and tied him off."

The banker frowned, leaning forward. "One of these Gauge men?" he offered, tentatively.

"Very likely. I'm already keeping a close watch on the rabble Harry Gauge brought into the area—we've established that the three who took down this bank were indeed our former sheriff's associates."

"And of course you'll be investigating the trollop," Carter said, tapping his desk with a fist, "this Pearl woman."

"I will." York stood. "You're the first I've told about Mr. Upton's murder, sir. Other than Doc Miller, of course. I figured you would want to break it, gentle, to those who worked with Mr. Upton."

Carter got to his feet. "Yes. Yes, I will. Thank you for that consideration. . . . You haven't interviewed my janitor yet. Would you like to borrow my desk again . . . ?"

"No, thank you, though," York said with an easy smile, tugging on his hat. "I'll take Charley somewhere for a talk . . . not the jail, I assure you. We wouldn't want to give the wrong appearance."

"No! Certainly not."

York checked on Charley, who was just finishing mopping up the area in back of the cashier windows. The janitor put his tools away and joined York, who walked him out of the bank and down the street to the Victory.

Hardly anyone was in there, and no one was drinking. But a bartender—not Hub, a stout fellow the sheriff didn't know by name—was behind the counter, sitting on a stool, having a cup of coffee, reading a dime novel about Buffalo Bill.

York leaned on the counter. "Could you rustle me up some of that Arbuckle's?" That was the brand of coffee everybody in town served. "And my friend here a beer?"

The bartender nodded, climbed off his stool, and went into the room in back of the counter. He returned with York's cup of coffee and then drew a beer for a grinning Charley, whose Adam's apple was bobbing in anticipation.

York guided Charley to a table among many empty ones, but as far from the counter as possible.

The sheriff said, "Seems like you had a real mess to clean up this morning."

"I surely did."

"That's unusual, isn't it?"

"Sometimes folks works late and brings food in and things gets spilt."

"Is that what happened last evening, you think?"

Charley had some beer. "Maybe. Whatever if it was, it shore took some elbow grease gettin' it offen that floor. It was sticky and where's it wasn't sticky, it was hard like peanut brittle. But I took enough soap and water after it, it's all shiny new again, the flooring."

"Well, that's good work, Charley. Did Mr. Carter call you in for that job?"

Charley nodded, grinning, Adam's apple bobbing. "He come to my room over the saddle shop and knocked. Early this morning. First time ever he come around hisself."

"Imagine that."

"Said there was a mess needs cleaned up before customers come round. And I said, shore."

Charley had some more beer.

"Charley, can you tell me anything about the robbery?"

Bony shoulders shrugged. "I wasn't there."

"Did you know about the bags of money in the safe?"

"What bags of money? Ain't they always bags of money in the safe? It's a bank safe."

"You didn't hear about a shipment of money through Wells Fargo?"

More beer as Charley thought that one over. "Wells and Fargo. That's the stagecoaches."

"Right. That's the stagecoaches. You hear anything about shipping money with them?"

"No, sir."

"Mr. Upton was killed last night, Charley."

Charley's mouth dropped. *"Whaaat?"*

"Somebody shot him and his body was found right back there." York pointed in the direction of the alley.

The janitor shook his head and kept shaking it. "Oh, that's terrible. That's just plain terrible."

"Did you like Mr. Upton?"

His head stopped shaking. "No, sir."

"Why's that?"

"He wasn't a nice man. He would push me sometimes. Push me out of his way. I'm bigger than him and that was dumb. I coulda done something back to him. But I'm an easygoin' feller. He called me slow! You think I'm slow, Sheriff?"

"Slower than some. Faster than others, I'd reckon."

"That's how I sees it. I hold down jobs all my life. Slow folk couldn't do that. Ain't no reason to push me out of the way and say mean things."

"How did the other bank employees feel about Upton?"

"Oh, they just kinder put up with him. I heard one say he was a cold fish. But lately he was . . . I wouldn't say *nicer,* but more easy to be around. He's got a lady friend now. Men with lady friends is in better moods. Till they marry them, anyways."

Charley had some more beer.

"How about Mr. Carter and Upton? Did they get along?"

"Far as it goes."

"They weren't close?"

"Close to what?"

"Friendly. Like father and son?"

"My father whipped me."

"I'm sorry to hear that, Charley."

"My ma loved me, though. She kilt my old man, with a shovel, and they come took her away. I was raised by a aunt. I guess I was close to her, the way you mean."

"Were Carter and Upton that kind of close?"

"No, sir. Just a boss and somebody worked for him. But . . . you know, lately, come to think—they been more friendly. I seen them smile and laugh together, just last week. Is that the kind of close you mean?"

"Might be," York said.

Charley finished his beer.

"You need me any more, Sheriff? I can make twenty cents this afternoon if I sweep out the saddle shop. Someday I'm gonna buy me one of them. I'm savin' for one."

"A saddle?"

"A horse. First things first, Sheriff." Charley finished his beer, grinned, and said, "Thank you kindly," and took his leave.

York sat drinking his coffee for a while. The strong stuff had been very hot when the bartender gave it to him, but York hadn't touched it during his conversation with Charley. Like Goldilocks said, now it was just right.

He didn't see her come over—not Goldilocks, but Rita Filley, who was suddenly just there, standing next to where he sat. She was wearing jeans and a yellow blouse and a red knotted kerchief at her slender neck, tooled cowboy boots too, a wardrobe right out of Willa Cullen's closet. She looked very young, no paint on her at all. Lovely child.

"Like it?" she said, nodding to the coffee. "Made it myself."

"You have skills that don't show," he told her.

"You don't know the half of it." She sat; she'd brought her own cup of coffee along. "You found a body behind my place, I hear."

"I did."

"You might have come in and told me about it. Last night. At the time?"

"I'm here now."

"So you are. But like I said, you could have—"

"I wanted to keep a lid on the murdered man's name, for just a little while."

The big brown eyes studied him. "Why would you do that?"

"To see how the dead man's boss reacted when I told him about it this morning."

"How did he react?"

"Oh, he was broke up about it. Even pretended to wipe away tears."

"Crocodile tears are the most common kind." She sipped her coffee. "So, then—now I'm free to spread the sad word?"

"Spread away. The dead man's Herbert Upton. The banker—or bank clerk, anyway."

She frowned. "Oh dear."

"A favorite customer?"

Staring into her coffee cup, she said, "No, he'd pretty much stopped coming here by the time I took over the place. But he used to be a regular, I understand. He and one of the girls here . . ."

"Pearl. I know her. Nice kid. Is she still working for you?"

Her eyes came up and met his. "That was . . . I guess it doesn't hurt talking about it now. Pearl told Upton she stopped working here. But she's still been coming in afternoons."

That much the bank president hadn't lied about, anyway.

Rita was saying, "Pearl's a popular girl, and she wanted to put a little money away before they got married."

"Build a little nest egg. Sleepin' with strangers."

"Not strangers. Regulars."

"What if it got back to Upton?"

She shook her head. "It wouldn't. It didn't. Those men Pearl was still seeing, last thing they'd want was a fiancé to

come steal her away, or shoot them or something. Damn."
She sighed. Shook her head. "I'll have to tell her."

He looked at the young woman who right now appeared
nothing like someone who might be running a place like
the Victory. "Would you do that?"

"Sure."

York let out a relieved sigh. "Wasn't lookin' forward
to that in the least."

"You think I am?"

CHAPTER TEN

The Purgatory River, a tributary of the Pecos, was a real godsend to Trinidad, not only a source of water and trout but of the most beautiful scenery for miles. The banks were lined with lush conifers, with splashes of orange and red from seasonal trees, and the water was cold and clear, flowing down from canyons in the Sangre de Cristo Mountains. Just above the rocky, sandy shore, where the river was around ten feet across, the grassy slope made a fine place for a picnic on a pleasant, sunny, not quite cool late morning.

Willa had accepted Zachary Gauge's request to go riding, and be shown "the sights" around Trinidad. Of course, in the immediate area, the sights were rather limited—range and cows, cows and range.

Eventually, if he proved horseman enough, she might take him into the hills and, atop buttes, point out how the blue-purple line of horizon went on forever as spiny desert shrubs and stubborn small trees wiggled in the wind. Would he see the beauty of those grassy plains, or discern only dust, thorns, and rock?

And if they made their way down, into those white-walled, blue-sky-ceilinged chambers, across a floor shared contradictorily by rock and green, would he see the stark majesty, or long for the man-made canyons of the city he left behind?

But if she'd been expecting a dude, she was surprised. His clothing was new, possibly bought locally at Harris Mercantile, though nothing overly fancy—gray wool California-style tight-waist/loose-legged pants, black sateen shirt, and black work boots. The fanciest things about him were the black, flat-brimmed, raw-edged, round-crown Stetson (minus the usual flashy feather) and, of course, that snowflake Appaloosa of his.

She had certainly not dressed up for him, not for a morning of riding, however easy she planned to take it on the Easterner—her usual ranch garb, red-and-black plaid shirt, jeans, work boots, her yellow hair braided up in a bun. The only thing approaching a fuss that she'd made was the picnic basket of food—cold fried chicken, pair of Mason jars filled with lemonade, some fresh biscuits (still warm when she packed them away), jars of honey, olives, pickles and jellies, and chocolate cupcakes.

Turned out he was a good, confident rider, and the only awkward moment was just before they left, when he gave her a look as she climbed up on Daisy.

"Something wrong?" she asked. The small picnic basket was slung over her saddle horn.

"No, I . . . I'm just used to ladies riding sidesaddle."

She might have been offended, but instead merely gave him a teasing little smile. "Maybe I'm not a lady."

The grin under his thin, well-trimmed mustache was nicely devilish. "Time will tell."

They spent several hours riding the range, where the beeves grazed and cowboys drifted through, keeping an eye on things. The men nodded to her and ignored the rider they assumed was a tenderfoot. For his part, Zachary seemed fascinated by the smallest things—a line shack, a barbed-wire fence, a roped stray—and took everything in, like a child eager to learn.

The sun wasn't quite above them yet when they settled on the slope above the sparkling river, the breeze a soothing third companion, and they ate the picnic lunch, very leisurely, sitting on an Indian blanket she spread out. He asked her a number of questions about the cattle business, some a little naive, most surprisingly smart, others just gathering information about this new world he found himself in.

"Why," he said, resting casually on his side, poised to have a bite of cupcake, glancing back at the glimmering river, "would they call a beautiful waterway like that 'the Purgatory'?"

Sitting Indian-style, she was working on a cupcake, too; she swallowed her bite before grinning mischievously, as she pointed in the direction the stream was running.

"Because Texas is that way," she said.

He laughed. "This country . . . such a hard place, but people still have a sense of humor."

"You have to have that," she said with a matter-of-fact shrug, about to take her last cupcake bite, "to survive."

"That's true everywhere." Zachary used a napkin on his fingers. "What an incredible feast. You may not have demonstrated yet that you're a lady, Miss Cullen, but you're clearly a woman of exceptional skills."

"Am I now?"

He nodded, and the expression on the handsome, vaguely Apache-like face was clearly admiring. "You ride like a man, you cook like an angel, and even in jeans and a plaid shirt, you're a vision."

She licked a crumb of chocolate cake from her upper lip, then said, "Maybe instead of establishing whether

I'm a lady should wait until we're determined whether or not you're a gentleman."

His laugh was hearty. "Please! I'm not getting fresh. You're quite safe with me, at least at the moment. I couldn't be more stuffed if a taxidermist had just finished with me."

She laughed a little herself. Then some silence settled in, which she broke by saying, "I gather you were pretty successful back East. On Wall Street, is it?"

He nodded. "I got in just after the war. My timing was good—they capped Stock Exchange membership in '69. It's not been an easy living—the security trade is prone to panics and crashes. That's one reason why I jumped at the chance to make a change."

"One reason, you say. Is there another?"

He smiled, but his expression was somehow melancholy. "Doesn't everyone who comes West have their reasons?"

"Personal reasons, you mean."

He shrugged slightly, avoided her gaze.

She said, "Forgive me, Zachary—I don't mean to pry."

He shrugged again and shook his head. "Miss Cullen . . . Willa. I just don't want to subject you to my sad story, and lead you to think I want you to feel sorry for me. I like you, Willa . . . not meaning to be forward. But your pity is not something I crave."

Willa knew she should let that stand—but how could she? How could anyone?

She leaned forward, smiled gently, and touched his hand. "Tell me."

He swallowed, and as he spoke, he looked past her. Into memory.

"Her name was Hannah," he said. "My childhood sweetheart . . . and later . . . my wife. She was very beautiful, as beautiful as you. But she wasn't strong like you. And the boy she gave me, Hiram . . . he wasn't strong, either."

The air between them had gone suddenly brittle, the breeze a little too cool.

She said, "They're . . . they're gone."

He swallowed again, nodded. "Diphtheria. Quite a bad outbreak in '81, back East."

She covered her mouth. Then her fingers lowered and she said softly, "I'm sorry. Zachary, I am so sorry."

His smile could only be described as brave. "My staff at the brokerage was exemplary. They covered for me for many, many months. They did very well without me, too, and when I finally returned, we did better still. And at work, I was fine. But at home, in our town house . . . too many memories. Too many ghosts. I tried moving, to an apartment on Park Avenue. Lovely place. I hated it."

His eyebrows rose.

"Then," he said, "a bolt from the blue . . . this golden opportunity courtesy of a black sheep who I barely knew. A fresh start. A new challenge. And here I am."

He told it so simply, so elegantly, with the tiniest smile, the heartbreak showing only in his eyes.

She was crying.

He came over and put an arm around her, and comforted her, as if the loss just described had been hers, not his.

"How selfish of me," he said, angry with himself, "to put you through that. I had no *right*. . . ."

She looked up at him and touched his face, her eyelashes pearled with tears, though the crying was over. Their faces were inches apart. Impulsively, she kissed him, tenderly, briefly, hand still touching his cheek.

They drew apart.

Emotions roiled through his expression like thunder in a sky swept black with clouds.

Then he kissed her, and it began as hers had, tenderly, but grew into something more, something passionate, something hungry. They kissed and they kissed, and he eased her onto her back and lay beside her, and his fingers found the buttons of her shirt. She raised a hand to stop him, but that hand froze in midair, and then his touch was on her underthings, cupping a breast, and his face was in her neck, kissing, nuzzling, loving, then lustful.

He seemed to catch himself and rolled off, turning his back to her. She flushed and did up her buttons and glanced away, ashamed. He was looking away as well, perhaps equally so.

"I'm sorry," he said, so soft the rush of the Purgatory nearly drowned it out. "That was . . . I'm *sorry.*"

Normal color returned to her cheeks and she slid over to sit beside him. She touched his hand.

"I don't mind," she said. "I really don't. But . . . it's a little fast, don't you think? A little sudden?"

He flashed her an embarrassed smile. "*Much* too sudden. *Far* too bold. I hope you can forgive me."

She smiled back. "Perhaps I should have fed you even more."

He laughed. "Perhaps all the blood is in my stomach, digesting that feast, leaving nothing in my head to help me think."

She had another idea about where that blood had rushed to.

"I suppose," he said, heaving a sigh, "we should be getting back. Your father might worry."

Willa waved that away. "No, we're fine. The Bar-O's a big spread. Papa will expect me to give you the nickel tour."

Zachary helped her pack up the picnic things, the folded blanket going in on top. They left the basket with their tree-tied horses, and they walked along the sandy, rocky shore, just taking in the scenic beauty.

At one point the Easterner stopped and she stopped, too, looking back at him. You could almost hear the water shimmer.

"I need to apologize," he said. "Not for how I feel. I can't tell you how wonderful it is for me to feel this way about a woman again. You've brought something alive in me that has been dead for . . . for a very long time."

"Zachary . . ."

"But I do apologize for . . . well, I know that things are moving too fast. But I've always been the kind of person who moves quickly to get what he wants."

She looked into the dark, almost Oriental eyes, and said, "I'm that kind of person, too."

He sighed, looked away, almost shyly. But then his gaze came back to her, hard and clear. "When the time is right," he said, "I want to talk to your father."

"About the ranch?"

"No." He shook his head. "That's all but decided. We'll be going over the legal documents soon. No, I need to talk to him about . . . us."

He might have tried to kiss her again, and she might have let him.

But he didn't, and she didn't encourage it. They just walked back to where the calico and Appaloosa waited.

Walked back hand in hand.

When he lost a hand because he wasn't paying attention, Caleb York decided it was time to throw in his cards—even though he was fifty-some dollars ahead. Two hours of poker, here at the Victory on another slow weeknight, had failed to keep his mind off his long, mostly unsuccessful day.

The day had started well, the interviews with bank president Thomas Carter and janitor Charley Morton, giving York a good idea of just how Herbert Upton came to die.

Before he met his Maker, the clerk had met his boss.

Carter had arranged to have his own bank held up, either to cover up embezzlement or simply to line his pockets with the townspeople's money. Upton had been an accomplice or perhaps a blackmailer—either way, it explained the clerk's recent promotion and raise.

So after hours, with no one else in the bank, Carter had shoved a pistol into Upton's belly and ended whatever problems the clerk had been causing. The bank president waited for the right moment—the sun had probably still been up when the murder was done—and after dark dragged Upton behind the Victory and dumped him in the alley there.

And janitor Charley had been woken up early before the bank opened the next day, honored by the president's presence on so lowly a doorstep, to come right now and clean up a sticky mess. Spilled food indeed.

As murders went, it was hardly the cleverest the ex–Wells Fargo detective had run into. If anything, the crime was a fairly clumsy one. But proving Carter guilty would take real doing. You didn't go around accusing one of the most respected city fathers of a cold-blooded killing, much less the robbery of his own bank, without utterly damning evidence. The circumstantial variety would never swing it.

So York had spent the late morning and the afternoon into early evening doing the kind of dogged, dull investigative work of which the dime novelists spared their readers. He talked to damn near everyone in town, at least those whose living quarters were above the Main

Street businesses. He, of course, never mentioned the bank president's name, merely asked whether anyone had heard a shot fired, or seen anything suspicious—say, someone hauling along a drunken friend somewhere. When he first got to the Victory this evening, York went around asking the same questions to the sparse clientele.

No one had heard anything.

No one had seen anything.

Nothing in the world pulls a lawman down worse than not being able to prove a guilty man guilty.

Dressed in his usual black, hat pushed back on his head, York had taken off his badge when he sat down at the poker table—always his habit, but somehow more significant tonight, perhaps because he was allowing himself to drink a little harder than usual. Before taking his seat at the poker table, in fact, he'd asked Rita to make sure he got the good stuff.

"Drinking yourself blind is one thing," York told her, with a nasty grin, "but going blind is something else again."

Rita, in a green satin gown with its usual low-cut front and up-the-middle slit, looked like a bowl of ripe fruit ready for the eating. But something in her face, especially around her dark eyes, seemed troubled.

"I always," she said, with a patient smile, "make sure you get the private stock. Straight from Denver."

"Thanks, honey."

She blinked at the familiarity. "Have you started drinking already, Sheriff?"

"No. Just a long damn day. Just a chasin'-my-tail wasted day."

She glanced around, though there were few patrons or even employees to see on this dead night. Then her eyes locked on his and she said, "I'd like to talk. Later."

"Sure. We can talk now if it's important."

He was aware that she lived on the premises, in the largest of the rooms upstairs.

She shook her head. "No. Enjoy yourself. Play some cards. Take a load off."

At Rita's nod, Hub the bartender gave York a bottle and a glass.

But during the time he sat playing cards—the ruffled-shirt house dealer accommodated him and played seven-card stud instead of the usual five-card—York had not put a dent in the bottle. Oh, it was the good stuff, all right, and no matter what Rita said, superior to the usual fare he was served here.

But his mind just would *not* let him enjoy himself. Wouldn't let him lose himself in the game, and drink himself into a better mood or for that matter a worse one. Two hours of this nonsense was enough.

When he rose, he glanced around for Rita, ready to have that talk with her. But she was nowhere to be seen. York went over to the counter and asked Hub if she was upstairs or in her office, and the bartender said, "No, Sheriff he went out half an hour or so ago."

"Say where she was going?"

"No. Sometimes she goes out for a walk, to just enjoy the night air. Go back to your game and she'll turn up soon enough."

York said no thanks and returned the largely unused bottle to the bartender.

Outside, the night air was nothing anybody would enjoy, not anything to go out walking in willingly—a wind had kicked up, and a cold one at that, and he had to snug his hat down to keep it from flying. The street was deserted, the jangle of his spurs the only sound besides the wind's hungry-wolf howl. Going on ten, few lights were on in the living quarters over stores, and only the faint glow of de Toro Rojo in the barrio, like a small piece of sunset that refused to go down, indicated anybody but the smattering of souls in the Victory were awake in this town.

At the hotel, the front desk was empty, attended only by a bell and a sign that said RING FOR SERVICE. The chinless clerk would be camped out in the office behind the wall of keys. The restaurant was dark, closed; the hotel, like the town, asleep. On this night, Trinidad was the kind of peaceful hamlet most sheriffs would relish—where a man with a star could pick up a paycheck for doing next to nothing.

Caleb York wished he could take the next stage out.

He trudged up the steps to his second-floor room, number 5. He had his key ready when he noticed the yellow light bleeding out from under the door. Taking a step back, and taking stock of himself—how much had he drunk? Hardly anything. He'd felt bone-tired before—how did he feel now?

Ready.

Or at least he did once the .44 was in his hand.

He turned the key fast to its click, then shouldered in but kept low, the big six-gun aiming upward.

"You really know how to make a girl feel welcome, Sheriff," Rita said, sitting in a chair by the window, near the kerosene lamp she'd lit on his dresser.

She was still in the emerald satin dance-hall outfit, the shelf of her full bosom uplifted by clever design, a long gray mannish coat hugging her shoulders. Her shapely legs were crossed and showing in their mesh stockings, extending boldly from the slit in the gown.

He rose from his near crouch, holstered the weapon, and shut the door behind him.

"A man's not allowed to have a female in his hotel room," York told her. "Unless he's married to her."

"Is that a proposal, Sheriff?"

"No. It's a city ordinance this hotel has to follow."

"We should find somebody official who can enforce that."

The room was small, the furniture sparse and nothing special. The green-painted iron bed would serve two. In case married people took the room. Nothing in the glorified cubbyhole said he'd lived here for six months, but he had.

"Are you drunk, Sheriff? How much did you drink?"

"I'm sober as hell and not thrilled to be. Never got around to emptying that bottle."

He went over and pulled the room's other straight-back chair over to sit and face her in the cramped quarters.

"You're in a mood, Sheriff," she said.

"I am at that."

"I don't suppose you'd care to share the reason why."

"There's a man who murdered another man, and I can't do a damn thing about it. For now."

"You could kill him."

"Not how I generally go about it."

Her smile had little to do with the usual reasons for smiling. "You're talking about the bank president and his clerk, aren't you?"

She said this as casually as if she'd asked him to pass a plate of biscuits, and don't forget the butter. He felt like he'd been slapped or maybe doused with water.

He frowned. "What makes you say that?"

"I see things," Rita said, shrugging, her half-exposed breasts taking the ride. "And I'm not stupid. Nobody else *has* a motive. He stole his bank's money, you think? Engineered it?"

After a moment, York nodded. "Carson had at least four accomplices. I killed three of them, and he killed the other, poor bastard."

"Pearl's back at the Victory."

Pearl, the prostitute Upton had planned to make an honest woman.

"What?" he said. "Working?"

"No, not working. Are you *sure* you're not drunk? I put her in a room upstairs at the Victory where she can cry her eyes out and feel sorry for herself and toss down her laudanum. She loved that little weasel. Or anyway she loved the respectability he promised."

"Upton was probably a blackmailer. How much does Pearl know?"

"Just that she's lost her chance at a different life."

"I want to question her."

Rita shook her head and her dark curls bounced. "Not tonight. Let her cry it out some. Anyway, she's in laudanum heaven by now."

He thought about that; then he looked at her. Hard. "Why are you here, Rita?"

"Not very flattering." She sighed. "I said I wanted to talk to you, and I do. But I didn't want to do it at the Victory."

"Why not?"

She ignored that. "I can't tell you where I heard this."

"Where you heard what?"

"Promise me you won't make me tell you where I heard this."

"I promise. *What?*"

Her eyes tightened. "That deputy of Gauge's you killed last April—Vint Rhomer. The one who beat my sister near to death before his boss finished the job. You killed him—right?"

"I did. I'd do it again. Gladly."

Rita smirked humorlessly. "Well, you're going to get the chance, in a way . . . unless you're smart enough to finally take a stage out of Trinidad."

"What are you talking about?"

She sat forward. "I mean, why is this *your* fight? You took care of those that shot down your friend Ben Wade. So walk away the victor. You must know that Thomas Carter is one of the most respected men in this community. Accuse him and they'll only fire you."

York was scowling at her. "What do you mean—get the chance to kill Rhomer again? What the hell are you talking about?"

She arched a dark eyebrow. "Did you know that Vint Rhomer was one of six brothers?"

"Yeah I do. They're all a bunch of low-down horse thieves, bank robbers, and murderers. Several rode with Harry Gauge."

"Well, they're riding again. Coming to Trinidad, sometime soon—don't know when exactly. But I know *why*—they're coming to kill you, Sheriff. All five of them."

His eyes tensed. "For revenge?"

"For revenge, but I think for money, too. Prospect of facing down Caleb York isn't something *any* man would take lightly, even with four other guns backing him up. You're a legend—remember?"

"I remember."

"So get out of town. Either that or find a dozen men you trust and arm them and put them in second-floor windows along Main Street. And when those five show up, shoot the Rhomers down in the street like the rabid dogs they are."

"I fight my own battles."

There was some sneer in her smile. "Well, of course you do. You're a legend. And pretty soon you'll *really* be a legend—like all good legends, like all good myths. You won't even exist."

He stood. Loomed over her. "Where did you hear this?"

She stood. Looked up at him. "I said not to ask. You promised."

He raised a fist. Shook it. "*Where,* Rita?"

Her teeth were small and white as she grinned defiantly at him, hands on hips. "Are you going to hit me, Caleb? Like Vint Rhomer used to hit my sister?"

His fist became limp fingers. He hung his head. "Maybe you should go."

"Maybe I should stay."

Her eyes were so dark, her lips so red, lush, wet, quivering. He went to kiss her and she met him halfway, her mouth like a blow to his face, a sweet, sultry slap, and his lips mashed against hers in response. Somebody's mouth was bleeding now. Both were breathing hard.

Rita turned the lamp down to the faintest glow.

Then, in the near darkness, she said, "You'll have to help me out of this thing—it hooks up in the back. I really do hope you aren't drunk, because this is going to take a man with talented fingers."

"Don't worry," he said.

CHAPTER ELEVEN

Mid-morning, with the sky clear and sunny, Caleb York was tugging his hat into place as he exited the sheriff's office when Whit Murphy, foreman out at the Bar-O, came spur-jangling up the steps onto the jailhouse porch. Lanky, bowlegged, of medium build, Murphy was a good cattleman, but he and York had butted heads from time to time.

"Good," Murphy said, his smile tight under the droopy, dark mustache. "Glad I caught you."

"I was just heading down to the telegraph office," York said with a gesture in that direction. "Why don't you walk along, and tell me what's on your mind?"

"If it's all right with you, Sheriff," Murphy said, "I'd druther talk right here, with no chance of nobody over-hearin'."

"Okay," York said. He pointed to two chairs on the porch and Murphy took one, and York took the other. The chairs were side by side, and Murphy sat on the edge of his, turning toward the sheriff.

"You and me," Murphy said, "any past hostilities is in the past, right?"

"That's where past hostilities go." He gave the edgy

man an easy grin. "When push come to shove, Whit, you backed me up. I don't forget that kind of thing."

"Good. Because I could use a friend right about now. Particularly a friend with a badge."

"Why so?"

Murphy took off his Texas-style Stetson and wiped his brow with the back of a wrist. While it was warmer today than yesterday, York figured the sweat wasn't much related to the temperature.

"Come to think of it," Murphy said, shaking his head, "it really ain't me that needs a friend. It's Miss Cullen."

Now York turned sideways in his chair. This wasn't just a bug up Murphy's backside—it was something real. Something serious.

"What's happened?" York asked.

"Nothin' yet—not quite. But we're right on the edge of the cliff lookin' down, and the horse don't like it one bit."

"Less poetry, Whit. More fact."

The foreman sighed, the big hat still in his hands, his dark hair as stringy and wet as if he'd been caught in a cloudburst.

"Sheriff," he said, "first thing this morning, that Zachary Gauge character shows up at the ranch house. Well, shows up ain't right. He was expected. That's damn near the worst part. It was a meetin' that Mr. Cullen agreed to, or maybe even set up hisself."

"What kind of meeting?"

"A real damn official one. Zachary wasn't alone. He had that lawyer, Arlen Curtis, with him. They had a passel of papers with them, and Mr. Cullen had rounded up a bunch of such items hisself. Deeds and titles and agreements. Miss Cullen was there—wearin' a dress!—and everybody was all smiles. Like it was a . . . a occasion."

"You saw them heading inside for this sit-down?"

York assumed this was something Murphy witnessed, while at the house on ranch business, on his way out to the herd and his cowboys.

But Murphy said, "No, sir, Mr. Cullen asked *me* to be there."

York frowned, not quite following. "Were you participating in some way, Whit?"

"Yes. Oh, nobody wanted my opinion. That would be the last thing they'd want. They just wanted me there as a witness. The lawyer needed somebody that wasn't either Mr. Cullen or Miss Cullen to sign them papers, too. Somebody who can read and write, and I fit the bill. So I sat there with them at that big table in the dining room."

"And did you sign your name as a witness?"

His sigh had some relief in it. "No, sir. Miss Cullen said she was surprised by the ... 'extend of the documents.' "

"*Extent* of the documents?"

"Yeah. Could be that's what she said. I guess she meant she didn't expect them to be a stack of papers thicker than *Ben-Hur*. She wanted to read them over on her own."

York shifted on the hard chair. "Do you think she had misgivings? This is all a little fast, isn't it?"

Murphy shook his head, sweat flying. "Well, it's goddamn fast, since you ask, but the Cullens sure didn't. All they wanted out of me was my John Henry here and there, only turned out I didn't have to give it yet. Lord knows I don't want to."

York tried again. "But was Willa ... wary about this partnership, or whatever it is, that Zachary Gauge wants her and her father to sign up for?"

He shrugged helplessly. "I don't rightly know. She's a smart gal and she don't want to sign nothin' that she ain't read over good. That don't make her suspicious."

"Are you, Whit? Suspicious?"

"Where that Zachary Gauge is concerned? Damn right. That guy is a snake-oil salesman if ever I saw one. Ten to one he's throwin' dust. But I'll give him this—he's good at it. Slicker than a greased pig."

"So when *will* they sign those papers?"

"Don't know. Probably tomorrow." Murphy sat forward so far, he practically fell onto the porch. "You got pull with Miss Cullen, York. You need to talk to her. She may listen to you. I tried. Didn't get nowhere."

York was shaking his head. "Whit, I'm afraid I don't have much pull left with the young lady. But I'll try. I will try."

He extended his hand and Murphy shook it. "Thanks for the tip, Whit."

"Don't mention it, Sheriff. We both care about the girl. But I think she's . . ." He swallowed thickly. ". . . think she's under that city bastard's spell."

The foreman got to his feet, slung on his hat, and jangled off.

York walked down to the telegraph office, mulling what Murphy had said. What the foreman shared had only added to his own suspicions.

Inside the small office, which wasn't much more than a counter, York filled out a form for a wire he'd intended to send even before Whit Murphy's cautionary visit:

TO PINKERTON'S NATIONAL
DETECTIVE AGENCY
NEW YORK, NEW YORK
ATTN: WILLIAM PINKERTON
BACKGROUND CHECK ZACHARY GAUGE
WALL STREET BROKER. URGENT. RUSH.
CALEB YORK, SHERIFF, TRINIDAD, NEW MEXICO

York handed the form to Ralph Parsons, the skinny, bespectacled operator behind the counter.

Skittish but friendly, Parsons said, "Thanks, Sheriff. You saved me a trip, stopping by—this just came in for you."

The telegraph operator handed York a wire, which he read right there.

TO SHERIFF CALEB YORK, TRINIDAD,
NEW MEXICO
RHOMER BROTHERS, LEMUEL, SAMUEL, LUKE,
LESTER, EPHRAIM, SEEN THIS CITY.
LEFT TOWN THIS A.M. HORSEBACK.
J. RUSSELL, SHERIFF, LAS VEGAS, NEW MEXICO

That meant the five outlaw brothers could be in Trinidad by this evening or early tomorrow.

York tucked the folded telegram in his breast pocket and gave the operator a two-bit tip. This pleasantly surprised Parsons, who rarely got a gratuity even when he delivered a wire, much less handed one across the counter.

But to Caleb York, the information in that particular wire was well worth paying for.

When he got back to the office, York found Tulley up and around, and making coffee. The sheriff had dispatched the erstwhile desert rat to patrol duty again last night, after which Tulley had settled in for forty winks or thereabouts on a cot in one of the cells. Sleeping in his clothes, recently store-bought though they were, gave the bearded, mussed-haired deputy a familiar disheveled look.

York got seated behind his desk and tossed the telegram casually on the desktop as Tulley delivered him a tin cup of coffee. The bandy-legged creature had learned one

thing, at least, sleeping under a desert sky all those years—
he made a damn decent cup of jamoka.

With company coming—even with York not knowing
exactly when—cleaning and oiling his .44 seemed on the
prudent side. He was seated doing that when Tulley stood
across from him and demanded to know what was in the
telegram. The reformed sot could not read, but he knew
damn well that wires didn't get sent "just for the merry
hell of it."

So York read it to him.

Going over the wire's simple if disturbing contents in
his mind, Tulley stumbled over to the scarred-up excuse
for a table that was as close to a desk as he was likely
ever to get, and plopped down. He sat brooding and sipping coffee.

Finally the deputy remarked, "Doesn't say they's
headed here."

"No it doesn't."

"But they's the brothers of that bastard Vint Rhomer,
y'know."

"Right."

"Vint Rhomer what you shot and kilt with that
very .44."

"Right again."

"So it might be they's comin' to wreak revenge on ye."

"Might be."

"Doesn't say as much in that there wire, do it?"

"Nope. But last night somebody tipped me off that the
Rhomers are headed here to settle up for what I did to
their brother. And rumor is they're being *paid* to do that,
to boot. Lucky break for them."

" '*Lucky break . . .*' " Tulley's chair screeched on the
plank flooring as he pushed it back and almost leapt the

distance between table and desk, where York was using a bore brush on the .44 barrel.

The deputy rested his weathered, stubby hands on the desk and leaned in. "Them five red-haired sons of a bitches is comin' to *kill* you, and you just sits there?"

"I'm not just sitting here," York said with a shrug. "I'm cleaning my gun."

Tulley went back and got his chair and dragged it over to sit across from the sheriff. "You need to tell somebody about this."

"I just did."

"Who?"

"You. You're my deputy. Remember?"

Tulley's face squeezed itself like a fist does a piece of paper about to be discarded. "No, *no,* I mean go to that citizens bunch what hired you, that mayor and them mucky-mucks. Tell them you need to put together a welcomin' committee of townfolk. Armed to the teeth!"

York shook his head. He was rubbing oil on the weapon with a soft cloth. "It's not their problem. It's mine."

Tulley's eyes were wild and his flaring nostrils were more suited to a rearing horse. "You ain't thinkin' this *through,* Sheriff. I know you are good with that dang thing, but five guns to one? Them is *terrible* odds! And if they does manage to cut down the great Caleb York, what do you suppose they'll do to this town after? It'll be a hellfire hoorah worse than any payday cowboys *ever* visited on poor ole Trinidad."

"If I'm not here," York said, with a small shrug, "then you're right—they'll have to step up and defend the town themselves. Long as I'm taking in breath, it's my job."

Tulley was on his feet now. "And there's where you're dead wrong . . . or, anyway, wrong. Best leave 'dead' out of it. It's *our* job, Sheriff. Said it yourself—I'm your deputy. You didn't give me that scattergun just to keep vermin out of the cell block. Referrin' of course to the crawlin' kind with tails and not the human kind, though plenty of them crawls, too."

York's eyes went from the gun he was cleaning to the deputy. "You want to back me up when the Rhomers come to town."

"I do. I aim to."

"And you know what breed of men these are. How lightly they take killing."

Tulley grunted deep. "I heard about 'em. And I seen Luke Rhomer kill two men over to Ellis, one of 'em the sheriff. The only reason they ain't hung the lot of them Rhomers is they leave precious few witnesses, and them that survives is scared to testify."

York was smiling faintly. "And you're still with me in this?"

"It's what ye pay me for."

"It's what the city's paying you for, Tulley."

Tulley threw his hands up. "City, then. Say I'm doin' it for the city and it has nothin' to do with helpin' out your sorry backside."

"Yes."

"Yes?" Tulley frowned. Blinked some. "*Yes,* like in . . . yes?"

"Yes, Deputy. But you won't be standing at my side like Doc Holliday if I wind up facing them down. It's back to the livery stable for you, Tulley."

The old boy's face bunched again. "My old job?"

York shook his head, snapping the .44 cylinder back in place. "No. *This* job. When that rabble rides into town, they'll come right past you there. I'll tell you what to do when the time comes. But you'll be in a position to see when they get here, and then come up behind them."

"You want me to *backshoot* 'em?"

"I don't care where you shoot 'em. If they're in this town to kill the sheriff, they don't get to cry foul."

Tulley almost glowed. Then he said, "When you're through with that oil and cloth and brush, could I borry 'em? I probably oughter give that scattergun some lovin' care."

"Sure, Tulley," York said with a grin, knowing the man hadn't even fired it yet.

Around three that afternoon, York entered the Victory, where a few cowboys leaned at the bar, each with a foot on the brass rail; one table of poker was going.

Rita, in dark blue satin finery similar to what he'd helped her out of last night, was standing toward the back by a table where three of her girls were sitting, waiting to be wanted. The boss lady was chatting with them and didn't see the sheriff at first; then one of the girls noticed him approaching and nudged her to look.

She came over quickly. "If you're here to talk to Pearl—"

"I am. She's had time enough to cry her eyes out and dope herself. Take me up there."

She huffed a sigh. "I wish you'd come up the back stairs."

"Why? Don't you want your patrons to know the sheriff is a regular? Might make them feel protected."

Her dark eyes were hard. "I just want to protect Pearl."

"Then I'll post a deputy or stick her in a jail cell."

Her frown was edged with anger. "No. Don't be a fool, Sheriff."

"I try not to be."

She was keeping her voice down. "I just mean . . . if you make a fuss over her, somebody may think she knows something."

"*I* think she knows something. Take me up there."

Reluctantly, Rita led him up the stairs at the rear of the saloon and onto the landing where half-a-dozen doors waited. Pearl was in the room at the far end over at left.

Rita knocked lightly and said, "I'm coming in, Pearl. Caleb York's with me."

The dance-hall queen waited for several seconds, to give the soiled dove the chance to make herself presentable, and then went in, York right after, shutting the door behind him. He'd been in this room once before, with Rita's sister Lola, a fact he saw no profit in sharing with the woman.

But it might have been any of the other rooms up here, except for the two-room suite where Rita herself camped out. The garish red-and-black San Francisco-style wallpaper made the small space seem even smaller; there was just room enough for a brass bed with a bedside table that was home to a hurricane lamp, which was casting a jaundiced glow, and a small dresser with a porcelain basin and pitcher. Also a chair for a cowboy to take his boots off and put them back on.

Under the sheet on the brass bed, like bundles of sticks, the skinny brunette in the white undergarment was a damn mess—her hair a tangle, her still-vaguely-pretty face, minus the paint, revealed as pockmarked and sunken-cheeked, with the big blue eyes the only real survivor among the nice features she'd started out with. A laudanum bottle was on the bedside table near the lamp.

He pulled the chair over and sat at her bedside, as if visiting a patient in a hospital, and this wasn't that different, was it? Rita, unhappy, stood at the door, her back to it, her arms folded.

"They killed my man, Sheriff," she said. The voice was as thin as she was. "Somebody should do somethin' about that."

"I'm going to," York assured her. "But I need your help."

"I'm too sick for that. Maybe tomorrow. He was so sweet to me. I knew he was special right off. I only let him pay me the first few times. We was gonna get married. Put all of this behind me."

He wondered if what she planned to leave behind included her laudanum habit.

"Pearl," he said, "I need to know if Herbert mentioned anything to you about his boss. Thomas Carter, the bank president."

"I know who his boss is. I can't tell you anything."

"You can't tell me anything because you don't know anything? Or because you're afraid to?"

"I can't tell you anything."

"If you're afraid, I can protect you."

Her smile was a crooked line drawn on her face by a child artist. "Herbert was a very sweet man. We was gonna move away from here. Now he's gone. Now I'm just a girl at the Victory again."

York sat forward. "Pearl, I think Mr. Carter may be responsible for Herbert's death. But right now, it looks like Carter may get away with it."

"He's an important man in this town."

"That's right. But it doesn't give him license to take a man's life. To take *your* man's life."

"Iffen I told you something, my man would still be gone. I would still be a girl at the Victory."

"If you know something, Pearl, you have to tell me. It's the only way for you to . . ." *What would work with her?* ". . . get even."

This smile showed teeth, yellowed but nicely formed. "Getting even don't bring Herbert back. That's gone from my life. Sheriff, I know you want to do right. But doin' right don't do no good. I'm sleepy now. Maybe we can talk later."

"Pearl . . ."

Rita's hand was on his shoulder. "That's enough," she said softly.

She was right.

York rose wearily, but when he got to the door, Pearl called to him.

"Sheriff—why are people afraid to die?"

He returned to her bedside, but didn't sit. "Because we don't know what's on the other side of that door, Pearl. Not for sure we don't."

"Is it heaven?"

"Might be." Of course Herbert Upton, if he were anywhere, would be in a warmer place. "You afraid to die, Pearl?"

"I am. I don't know why, because bein' a girl at the Victory, that's no kind of life. But the way Herbert got shot, that hurt him, didn't it? Bad. Did he take a very long time to die?"

"I'm afraid so, Pearl."

"So I should help you make the person who did that die, too. Maybe die just as bad."

"He'd hang. That's plenty bad."

The big blue eyes stared up at him; they were truly

beautiful. "Maybe being dead ain't what scares me. Maybe it's the time it takes doing it. The dying?"

"Let me protect you, Pearl. Tell me what you know, agree to testify, and I'll—"

But now the eyes had closed. She was not dead, just sleeping. Just riding the laudanum cloud like an angel.

CHAPTER TWELVE

Around six o'clock, with the day's sun still sliding into evening, a clerk from Harris Mercantile came by the jailhouse with word from Mr. Harris.

The towheaded youth—maybe sixteen—was the shopowner's middle boy. He'd never been in the sheriff's office before and his eyes were big with the gun rack and wanted posters as he said, "Pa says the Citizens Committee is about to convene. They request you attend, with due respect."

Caleb York—seated not at his desk but by the barred window onto the street, should the Rhomers make good time on their ride from Las Vegas—said to the boy, "That 'due respect,' son—are they giving it, or am I to bring it?"

"Sir, I don't know, sir. I just know they want you."

"I'll be right down."

The boy nodded, looking around all big-eyed, taking in the first of the cells before the others disappeared out of sight behind the far wall.

"Sheriff, how many cells you got back there?"

"How many do you need?"

The boy blinked at him.

York smiled. "Four cells. We accommodate four to a cell, if called for."

"What if there was more bad people than sixteen?"

The boy had math skills.

"Well, then," York said, "I guess I'd just have to shoot the excess."

The boy's eyes got even bigger, he swallowed, and scurried out.

York got up, tied his .44 down just in case, went out, and locked the door behind him. As he began to walk down to the mercantile, he nodded over to Tulley, out in front of the livery stable, leaning on a broom.

The deputy, who nodded back, would appear to anyone riding in—the Rhomers, for instance—just a harmless coot doing odd jobs at the livery. Few if any would notice the scattergun leaned up against, and mostly hidden, by the nearby blacksmith anvil.

The sign said CLOSED in the window of Harris Mercantile, but the door was unlocked. A meeting was already under way in back, past the front two-thirds of the store, and just beyond the wood-burning stove. Perhaps a dozen chairs were arranged in two semicircular rows, leaving an aisle between; the seating faced the same slightly raised table used on occasion by the circuit-court judge.

Is this a trial? York wondered. *And am I the defendant?*

At that table, in the judge's chair, sat Jasper Hardy, the town's fastidious little barber mayor, gavel in hand, with elaborately well-dressed banker Carter seated up there at His Honor's left, their host Newt Harris to his right.

Curl-brimmed hat in hand, the black-clad sheriff moved down the aisle past the other city fathers—druggist Clem Davis, hardware man Clarence Mathers, telegraph manager Ralph Parsons, undertaker Perkins, among others—and took a seat right in front.

York knew he must be a topic of discussion here—perhaps *the* topic—because he normally wasn't invited to these meetings. So he positioned himself where they could have at him. If they had the grit.

Too late he realized he was sitting right across from Willa, seated next to her father, with Zachary Gauge on the other side of the old man. She wore a blue-and-white calico dress and her hair was down, blue-ribboned back—she looked nothing like a tomboy this afternoon. They exchanged nods and polite, awkward smiles.

The smile the mayor gave to York was similarly polite and even more awkward. "Sheriff, we're glad to see you here. Thank you, sir, for accepting our invitation."

Why? he thought. *Is it a dance?*

The room was already pin-drop quiet when the mustached mayor pointlessly banged his gavel a couple of times, then contradicted the formality of that by addressing York again.

"Sheriff," Hardy said, "please understand—this isn't an official meeting."

York said, "Could have fooled me."

"The committee members did meet just half an hour ago," the mayor went on, "and while no vote was taken on the subject, we were in general agreement that it would be best for Trinidad . . . and in *your* best interests, too . . . if you were to step down from your post."

"That's my intention," York said, in a voice both quiet and strong, "when a certain matter is resolved."

"If I might, Jasper," Thomas Carter said to the mayor. Then the banker's gaze went to those watching, though not landing on York. "I believe this concerns me as much, if not more, than anyone here."

Then, with the kind of sincerity only a crooked bank president could muster, Carter smiled down at York and said, "We all appreciate everything you've done for Trinidad. Your quick response to the robbery of First Bank took down two of the scoundrels right at the scene, and, of course, you tracked down and shot and killed their ringleader. You even returned a portion of the stolen funds. A small portion, granted, but nonetheless a gesture appreciated by me . . . by all of us."

"You're welcome," York said dryly.

"But it seems unlikely that you will be able to recover the rest of the stolen funds. . . ."

"I have a pretty good idea where they are."

The banker flinched, smiled nervously, and went on, "Be that as it may, the city of Trinidad no longer requires your services."

"Oh," York said, his surprise clearly feigned, "you want me to step down *now*? Not let the door hit me in the tail on the way out, you mean?"

A few chuckles came from those seated behind the sheriff.

"We do," the banker said firmly. "Our, uh, relative haste has a practical basis, as you well know."

You mean, York thought, *the longer I stay, the more likely I'll nab* your *well-dressed ass?*

But York said, "I'm afraid I don't know. You'll have to educate me."

The banker sighed and turned to the mayor with an exasperated expression. "Jasper? Please. Explain to the man."

The little barber said, "We learned earlier today that five very dangerous men are riding from Las Vegas to Trinidad to . . . how best to put it? Do battle with you, Sheriff. To engage in the kind of shoot-out that gave Tombstone such a black eye."

"Their names are Rhomer," York said, in a clear, loud voice. "Brothers—very dangerous, yes. You'll all recall our ex-sheriff Harry Gauge's brutal deputy, Vint Rhomer. I shot him down like the animal he was at the relay station last April. Many of you here thanked me for that."

Willa's head was lowered.

"I can well understand," York said, "that you don't want Main Street turned into a shooting gallery. Neither do I. But I do have one question."

Up on the raised table, the mayor, the banker, and the mercantile owner glanced at each other. Then Hardy asked York, "What question is that, Sheriff?"

York turned and looked at skinny, four-eyed Ralph Parsons. "Since when did Western Union start making the contents of their telegrams public?"

Parsons gulped and lowered his gaze; his derby was in his hands and he was turning it like a spigot he wanted to shut off.

"Those men," York said, addressing them all, "could be here at any moment."

The banker snapped, "That's right! So you need to pack up your things and saddle your horse and go, while there's still time."

With a frustrated sigh, Harris said, "Sheriff, nobody appreciates what you've done for this town more than we do. But the last thing Trinidad needs is a big showdown like the one promised by these five notorious killers."

The mayor said, "But if they come to town, and find you gone, they'll move on. No harm done."

Willa almost shouted: "They'll move on, all right, and go after Caleb! What's *wrong* with you people, anyway? Aren't there any *men* in this room?"

A warm feeling for the girl flowed through York, but as if in answer to her question, Zachary Gauge sprang to his feet. He was in the black frock coat that made him look half preacher, half gambler.

"Miss Cullen's words ring true," the Easterner said. "We should be banding together to help the sheriff stave off these outlaws. They are five—we are a whole blasted town. If the Rhomers ride in, expecting to find one man and instead find themselves facing a well-armed community, why, they'll scatter to the four winds like the cowards such men always are."

A smattering of applause.

Old man Cullen shouted, "You people should be *ashamed*! Caleb York is the best damned thing that ever *happened* to this town."

More applause, not just a smattering.

"I demand a vote on this issue!" the banker said, just shy of yelling, his fist raised like it was the gavel.

The mayor said, "We'll take a vote. . . . Sheriff, is there anything else you'd like to say before we do?"

"Only that while I appreciate my friend Zachary here, for expressing his sentiments, I am not asking you good people to stand behind me with anything but moral support. I'll take your prayers but not your guns."

Frowning, Zachary said, "But one man alone—"

"Sir, I'm not alone."

The banker snorted. "What, that desert-rat deputy of yours? You must be joking."

"I can handle this. There are only five of them."

Harris said, "Five *guns*, Sheriff."

"Five guns. In the hands of five louts."

More chuckles, more scattered applause.

"Mr. Carter," York said affably, "look at it this way— if they shoot me down, you won't have to fire me. Hell, you won't even have to pay me my last month's salary."

They voted.

The bank president's was the only hand raised in favor of removing Caleb York from the office of sheriff.

As Carter was stepping down from the table, York was right there. "Mr. Carter, I have a comment."

"I have no interest, sir, in hearing it."

"Here it is, anyway. If one of us needs to leave town in a hurry, it isn't me."

York smiled pleasantly, put his hat on, tipped it to the banker, whose face had gone pale, and started out.

But then Zachary, in the aisle just ahead of York, turned, a big smile under the thin mustache in his narrow, well-carved face.

"If you handle the Rhomers," Zachary said, in a near whisper, "half as well as you did that banker, none of us have anything to worry about."

And Zachary extended a hand, which York shook.

"I appreciate you standin' up for me," York told the man.

Zachary's smile disappeared and something thoughtful took its place. Something . . . troubled.

"Might we have a word in private?" Zachary asked.

"Sure."

The two men walked away from where many of those in attendance were lingering, talking in smaller groups.

Over by a wall, Zachary said, "You once recommended I take the counsel of my Circle G foreman, Gil Willart."

"Well, if I did, I shouldn't have put it so strong. Willart was one of your cousin's men, though he's no outlaw. Strictly a cattleman. I just thought he might be useful in pointing out the bad apples still in your crop."

"I'm afraid," Zachary said, frowning, "Gil may *be* one of those apples. My understanding is that this Rhomer gang is coming in from Las Vegas."

"Yes, sir. That's been confirmed."

"Well, Gil spent two days in Las Vegas this week, looking into buying cattle for me. Is that a coincidence?"

"Could be."

"And I know he's been thick with these roughnecks my cousin Harry brought in, may he not rest in peace." Zachary shrugged. "Just thought you should know that this Willart may not be an ally."

"Appreciate it," York said with a nod.

Zachary nodded back, and went over to where Willa had been waiting. They spoke briefly and then she came over to York.

"Caleb," she said, smiling, less awkwardly now, "while there's part of me that *does* wish you would leave before these outlaws come to town...I am very happy that things this afternoon went the way you wanted."

"Thank you, Willa. And thanks for sticking up for me."

She swallowed. Nodded shyly. "You deserve no less. And I'm so pleased that you and Zachary are getting along so famously."

"Seems to be a good man."

"I'm glad you feel that way. Because...you have a right to know this...he and I are engaged to be married."

York said nothing. It was tough to talk after a blow to the belly like that. But he did find a smile, and so did Willa, before she joined Zachary and exited with him, arm in arm, following her blind father out.

York walked up to the livery, where Tulley was sitting on the anvil, smoking a cheroot that smelled only a trifle worse than the crapped-on straw in the stable behind him.

"Seen all kinds of folks head in the mercantile," Tulley remarked. "You was about the last of 'em. Am I wrong sayin' it looked like an indoors hangin' about to commence?"

"It almost was. Any doubt I had about that bank president killing his chief cashier? Just rolled out of town like a tumbleweed."

York filled his deputy in on the meeting, including Willa's surprise announcement of her engagement to Zachary Gauge.

"That feller moves faster than a Texas twister," Tulley said. "You trust him?"

"He stood up for me."

"Tryin' to look good, y'think?"

"Mebbe. Tulley, when it gets along about midnight, there's scant chance the Rhomers will ride in. And if they do, doubtful they'll be lookin' for trouble, at that hour."

Tulley nodded emphatically. "Gunfights in the dark ain't good for nobody. I don't think we'll see them sidewinders till after sunup."

" 'Sidewinders'?"

"*Sidewinders*. Them's rattlers, and a word suited for the likes of the Rhomers."

"I know what a 'sidewinder' is, Tulley. I just want to make you know your job isn't 'town character' anymore. You're a deputy now."

"Well, this deputy could use some shut-eye."

"Come midnight, camp out under that window over there." York pointed toward the livery stable. "You hear anybody ride into town, wake up like a real rattler crawled up your pant leg."

Tulley nodded. "You sleepin' in the jailhouse tonight?"

"No. I made arrangements to bunk in over there." He pointed to the nearest shanty of a pueblo in the barrio. "So you know what to do?"

"I know."

"Once you've done it, scramble back in that livery and take cover. They could come after you."

"They do, and we'll have 'em in a squeeze, won't we?"

"That's the idea. One of the ideas, anyway."

A big toothy grin blossomed in the white beard. "People gonna write about this, ain't they? Ned Buntline and them dime-novel authors."

"Yep. The trick is to be alive to read 'em."

Tulley closed one eye and jabbed a finger at him. "You stay alive, too, Caleb York. I needs somebody to read 'em *to* me."

York walked down to the Victory Saloon, where business was a little better tonight but still nothing to get excited over, and found Rita at the bar in conversation with Hub.

"A word?" York said to her.

In a red-and-black satin number, she shrugged and led him to a table in an empty area of the saloon. They both sat.

She said, "I hear the Citizens Committee tried to give you the boot. And you talked them out of it. I never took you for the slick type, Sheriff."

He ignored that. "How's Pearl doing?"

"Better today. I'm backing her off on her bottle of happiness. She's talking about going back to work."

"What kind of work?"

Rita smirked. "The kind you think. If I can wean her off that laudanum, I might be able to keep her on here, after I shut the brothel down. She'd be a right pretty girl with some meat on her, and if those dark bags under her eyes would pack up and leave."

Hub brought his boss a Mule Skinner and York a beer.

York sipped the warm brew, then asked, "She have other special male friends, besides that bank clerk?"

"None that want to marry her. Several that saw her regular."

"Would one of them be Gil Willart? Foreman out at the Circle G?"

Her glass froze halfway to her lips. "Why do you ask that?"

"Playin' a hunch. You know Willart? Never mind Pearl—is he a regular here?"

A tiny shrug. "He comes in, time to time."

"You know, I believe I've seen him in here myself. I might even put it stronger than 'time to time.' "

A bigger shrug. "Put it however you like it, Sheriff. It surprise you, we got cowboys around here who are regulars? Who else did you think we catered to?"

He sipped beer. "Gil Willart was in Las Vegas for a couple days this week, on Circle G business."

"Fascinating, the information you lawmen pick up."

"Speakin' of that, I received a wire today from the sheriff in Las Vegas, warning me the Rhomers are heading to Trinidad. Packing five bullets with my name on 'em. Knowin' the Rhomers, all misspelled."

Her expression was bored, or pretended to be. "Should I stop you when this starts having anything to do with me or the Victory?"

"Don't bother. We're almost there. What the sheriff in Las Vegas *didn't* tell me was that the Rhomers are hired guns in this. That somebody paid them to take their vengeance out on me. Oh, that's right—*you* told me, Rita."

"Did I? I forget. I run at the mouth sometimes. Bad habit."

Another sip of beer. "You wouldn't tell me who told you, as I recall. I'm guessing it was Willart."

She said nothing.

He grinned at her. "Think we just got there, didn't we? The place where this starts to have somethin' to do with you, Rita, and this place."

She said nothing.

"It was Gil Willart who told you the Rhomers were coming after me. Because it was *Gil Willart* who hired them to do it."

She winced as if he were being so stupid, it hurt. "Why would Gil hire somebody to kill you?"

"Because somebody told him to. That bank president, maybe. Now tell me this—why didn't you want to say Gil was who told you? You're not a priest. What's betraying that kind of confidence to you, anyway?"

"Sheriff . . . Caleb. . . ." She sighed and touched his hand. *My God, her eyes were wet!* "There's some things you shouldn't ask me. There's some things I shouldn't tell you."

"Let me tell *you* something then—no 'ask' about it. That bank president, or some accomplice of his, murdered Pearl's intended. And that bank clerk could be just the first, should there be other loose ends that need snipping. Are you one, Rita? Is Pearl?"

She drew her hand back. "Caleb. Please don't."

"I want to put her in a jail cell."

"Pearl didn't *do* anything!"

"I know she didn't. I want to protect her. You should be in the cell next to her, and whether you did or didn't do anything, I want to protect you, too."

Those dark eyes *were* wet. "Why do you want to protect me?"

"Because I'm the sheriff."

"Not the man who saw me in the glow of lamplight?"

"I'm him, too. We both want to protect you."

She swallowed thickly. Sighed deep. Her lashes fluttered like tired butterflies.

Then she said, "He's here right now."

York sat up. "*Who's* here right now?"

"Gil Willart."

"What the hell . . . ?"

"He was worried about Pearl. He's one of her regulars, I told you. One of her . . . special men."

York looked at her, disgusted. "You mean, he's up there right now, bouncin' on the bedsprings with that sick kid?"

"No, no, no. He cares about her. Truly cares. He just wanted to check on her, talk to her. . . ."

York was out of his chair and halfway across the room in seconds. He started up the stairs and then, heading down them, came a cowboy in dusty chaps and a green-striped silk shirt and a hat so battered its original shape was a mystery. He was of medium size with an oversized mustache, and his squashed oval face was home to leathery skin and green eyes.

Gil Willart.

For a moment, the two men froze, each with a hand hovering over a holstered six-gun.

York tried to calm the situation. "Just need a word, Gil. Just a word."

Right hand still poised to draw, York gestured with his left for Willart to keep coming. When they were on the same step, the two men walked slowly down, side by side, and then over to an empty table toward the front.

York and Willart sat across from each other. The weathered foreman looked glum.

"How's Pearl doing?" York asked.

"She's gonna be okay. Purty blue right now. Been through plenty."

"You like the girl."

"I do."

"Maybe you'd like to take her away from all this."

"What d'you mean, Sheriff?"

"Maybe give her a better life."

"I'm a damn cowboy."

"So, you weren't jealous? Of Upton?"

The green eyes in the leather mask flared. "That pipsqueak! Hell, no. If he wanted to marry her, that was jake with me. Pleased to see her catch a break."

"You wouldn't have minded that? Her going off and marrying somebody else?"

The cowboy shook his head. "No. Why, you think *I* belly-shot that clean-nails bastard? No, sir. I wasn't even in town."

"That's right, Gil. You were in Las Vegas."

Willart shifted casually. "I was at that. Lookin' into buying some cattle for my new boss."

"Didn't happen to run into the Rhomer boys while you was there, did you?"

The foreman frowned. "What's Rita been tellin' you, anyways? You know you can't believe nothin' these whores come up with."

"Call Rita a 'whore' again, Gil, and I'll hand you your teeth."

York waved Rita over.

"Yes?" she said.

"Check on Pearl," York said. "If she's up to comin' down, put a robe on her and bring her. If not, tell her we're comin' up to talk."

Rita shook her head. "Can't you leave the poor kid alone?"

"No."

She sighed and trudged off.

"Gil," York said pleasantly, "if I find out you hired the Rhomers to come and kill me, I'll consider that right unfriendly."

Willart worked up a sneer. "And you'll kill *me* like you killed so many?"

"Most likely, yes. Now my thinking is, you don't have enough against me to hire those Rhomers yourself. You'd be doin' it for somebody else. That banker maybe."

"I'm listenin'."

York shrugged. "Well, in that case, I'd be way madder at who give you that task than at you for carryin' it out. I might even trade your worthless goddamn life for such information."

Willart was thinking about that, green eyes moving, when the scream came from upstairs.

A woman's scream, it ripped the quiet night at the Victory apart like a piece of cheap cloth. York and Willart both jumped to their feet, looking up in the direction of that terrified howl.

Rita was on the landing in front of the doors to the dance-hall girls' cribs, leaning on the railing, her face white, her eyes huge, the red mouth in the pretty face distorted into something ugly.

"It's Pearl!" she cried.

"Come with me," York said to Willart, but he needn't have bothered, because the cowboy was just behind him as they both bounded up the stairs.

The door to Pearl's room stood open, the way Rita had left it.

The skinny brunette was sprawled on the bed, still half under a sheet, much of that sheet stained scarlet now, the girl's head back too far, in a position made possible by whoever slashed her throat ear to ear, creating a gaping, grinning second mouth. The blood had run down the front of her white nightgown, like her body was crying for her, but she was dead, so it wasn't flowing now.

York instinctively turned to Willart, whose horrified

expression turned to fear as he shoved York, hard, and took off running.

York followed the cowboy out onto the corridor of the landing. Gasps and cries came up from the patrons below. Willart ran down the stairs so fast that he stumbled a third of the way from the bottom, somersaulting the rest of the distance, and when the cowboy got to his feet, he found himself facing Caleb York, halfway down the steps by now.

"Don't!" York said, holding up his left palm, and stopping where he was.

But Willart went for his gun, and it hadn't cleared its holster when York's two .44 bullets ripped through him, shaking him, making him do the saddest little dance, as blood shot out his back in twin streams, before he crumpled on legs that, no matter how bowed, just couldn't hold him up anymore.

CHAPTER THIRTEEN

The explosive reports of his .44 were still echoing and reverberating in the high-ceilinged saloon when—still several steps up from the man he'd just shot—Caleb York said, "Damn."

He went down those last few steps and knelt by Gil Willart, knowing the man would be dead but checking anyway. Rita was making her way slowly down the stairs, leaning a hand on the banister all the way down. Her face was white as a lace hanky.

She paused on the step from which York had fired, asking, "Did you have to kill him?"

Slowly, York got to his feet. "I wish to hell I hadn't. He died knowing things I need to."

The dark eyes were big and round. "Why *did* you then? You shot him *twice,* Sheriff. If you wanted him alive . . ."

"A man pulls on me, I put him down." He glanced at her. "That's how I can be standing here jawing about it with you."

She drew in a breath, nodded. But she stayed where she was on the stairs, the garish beauty of her dance-hall attire at odds with the crumpled shot-to-hell cowboy at its foot.

York asked the woman, "Were any of the other rooms up there occupied?"

She shook her head. "No. None of the girls was doing any . . . entertaining this evening."

"Well, we need to clear this place out," the sheriff said, but when he turned to look, the clientele had already skedaddled. All that remained were one bartender and the dealer at the poker table, as well as the girls at the table back near the empty dance floor and unmanned piano. The doves looked ashen and afraid, and one was crying. They'd clearly seen Willart die, and even in a room this size, the bouquet of gunpowder lingered.

Finally getting around to holstering his .44, York went over to the bar and told Hub to stand guard at the batwing doors. For now, the Victory was closed. The big bartender did this without comment or question.

Then York went over to the poker table and told the gambling man who dealt there to go fetch Doc Miller.

The dealer, Yancy Cole, wore a white round-brim black-banded hat, a gray suit, and a ruffled shirt. It was the kind of outfit that got you killed if you weren't a gambler, and sometimes got you killed, anyway.

In a Southern accent that might have been real, Cole said, "Perhaps the unduh-take-ah might be the bettah party to bring around."

"We won't have to send for the undertaker," York said. "He should be here anytime now."

The sheriff had barely spoken those words when the bartender at the doors let in a little man all in black—*did Perkins sleep in those mourner's duds?*—and came over in a solemn one-man procession. He had his black beaver high hat in hand, revealing a head bald as an egg, and he was skeleton skinny under that frock coat.

Perkins stood near the corpse and said to York, "Has the deceased any family?"

"Not that I know of. Likely be the usual two dollars paid by the city."

The undertaker nodded. Such bad news was as inevitable as death itself.

"But there's another two dollars upstairs," York said encouragingly. "One of the girls here. Murdered."

"By this gentleman?"

"I don't believe so. But I don't want any of the bodies dragged off just yet. I have some detective work to do here first."

Hub was letting Doc Miller in. Based upon the rumpled state of his brown suit, and his uncombed white hair, the stubby little medic probably *did* sleep in his clothes.

The doc, Gladstone bag in hand, trundled over and raised a white eyebrow at the corpse, then turned his gaze to the undertaker and raised the other one.

"Mr. Perkins here has the right idea," Miller said. "There appears to be nothing more to be done for this poor creature but to bury him."

"Agreed," York said, then gestured a thumb at the ceiling. "And you've lost *another* patient upstairs."

York filled the doctor in.

Having absorbed it all, Miller nodded toward the undertaker. "That also sounds more like this gentleman's purview than my own."

"No, Doc, I want you to bring your medical eye to the murder room."

That seemed reasonable to Miller, who followed the sheriff up the stairs, Rita having already gone back up to the landing, where she paced a small area, arms folded.

As the two men stood poised at the doorway of Pearl's

little room, the doc said, "Well, our dead friend down-stairs didn't do this."

"I know he didn't."

"Then my medical eye may not be needed. How did you come up with that diagnosis, Caleb?"

York gestured. "Headboard's against the wall. The girl's killer faced her. Left side of the bed, I'd say. A throat slashed like that bleeds all to hell. Willart would have been covered in the stuff."

Miller nodded. "Well-reasoned. He'd have been sprayed head to thigh. Whoever did this went out dripping."

"Good point. Keep lookin', Doc, I'll be back right quick."

York moved out onto the narrow strip of landing be-tween wall and railing. The flooring had a runner of car-pet, dark red, and on close inspection, drops of similar red indeed could be made out. They led to the doorway onto the rear stairs that emptied out into the alley where not so long ago Tulley had found the body of Pearl's bank-clerk fiancé.

Those stairs were bare wood and all the way down a trail of red drops, tiny splashes where they hit, led to the door and then out into the alley. There the killer had mocked York by dumping something between those two garbage barrels, right where Upton had been found.

A duster, the front of the tan light-linen coat drenched in Pearl's blood, still shimmering with it, lay crumpled, discarded, like a skin a snake crawled out of.

Well, hadn't one?

A tossed handkerchief was covered in blood—the killer had wiped his face off, since that much flesh at least had been exposed to the scarlet spray.

York could see where somebody had scraped the bot-tom of their shoes the way you would deal with muddy soles before heading inside. Smears of blood were dug into the wavy, heavy shoe marks, and no droplets led away from the alley at all.

A cold-blooded killing had taken place in the very building where—and while—York had been questioning Gil Willart. That is, the killer's blood had been cold— Pearl's was still warm. But the sheriff had no doubt that when Willart left Pearl, she'd still been breathing.

This had just happened.

And the killer had slipped away, out the back door, like a cheating husband.

Right under York's damn nose.

Heaving a sigh of self-disapproval, York trudged up those back stairs and soon was with the doctor in the murder room again.

"She died quick," the doc said. "Horribly, but quick. One of those small favors we're expected to thank God for."

"What else can you tell me?"

The doc pointed to the floor near the bed. "Look under there. That's the murder weapon."

York nodded. "I spotted that, but haven't had a close look yet."

"Take one."

York did.

The knife was small, the kind usually tucked into a boot or belt or sleeve, five inches of pointed blade with a jigged bone handle and double brass guard—dagger-style, its gleaming double-edged blade looking razor sharp. One side of the blade bore tiny tears of blood.

"Smoky Mountain toothpick," York said, rising.

"So sharp," the doc said, "it made its cut and took just a little blood away with it."

York pointed at the dead girl. "What does the wound tell you, Doc?"

"That's a right-to-left wound, judgin' by the messy exit point. Probably a right-handed man, but that's nothing you can take to a jury. That kind of blade? You can swing backhanded, if you've a mind."

York nodded. "Step into the hall, would you, Doc?"

They spoke just outside the murder room. The sheriff told the doctor of the bloody trail down the steps and the blood-spattered duster they led to.

"I could use some help gatherin' the evidence, Doc. Grab a sheet off of one of these beds and go down and wrap that bloody duster up for me, and keep it at your office till I need it."

The doc gave him half a humorless smile. "You figure that's a good place for it, do you? Since I get more blood splashed around in my surgery than you do in your office."

York gave him a grim smile. "I knew you'd understand."

The doc nodded toward the murder room. "You want me to secure that weapon?"

"No, I'll get it."

York went back in, picked up the Smoky Mountain toothpick, wiped what little blood there was off on the bedsheet, and stuck it in his boot, where there was a place for such a weapon.

Then, standing tall, he looked down at the poor dead girl, her mouth frowning, her wound grinning, the skinny thing all blister pale.

"I'll get the son of a bitch, Pearl," he told her quietly. "Don't you worry a hair on your pretty little head about it."

York returned to the main floor of the saloon, where near the bottom of the stairs the undertaker stood guarding his two dollars.

"Go on and get your wicker baskets, Mr. Perkins," York said. "They're all yours, upstairs and down."

Perkins gave him a ghastly smile. "You're a good man, Sheriff."

"One thing, Mr. Perkins."

"Yes, sir?"

"Those outlaws comin' to town after my hide?"

"Uh . . . what about that, sir?"

"If things don't go my way, and you put me in your window? I will haunt your skinny backside till Judgment Day."

Perkins gulped and turned as white as the dead girl upstairs. "Sir, I would never. . . ."

But York, smiling darkly to himself, had moved on to where Rita was keeping her upset girls company at their table toward the back.

He took her aside. "Honey, you need to pack a bag."

She frowned, startled by the suggestion. "What?"

"Not everything you own. Just enough to hold you over for two or three days."

"What for?"

He brushed a tendril of dark hair from her face. "I aim to protect that girl I saw in the lamp glow the other night."

That stopped her. She smiled just a little. "So you *do* care?"

"A sheriff cares about every citizen. Some a little more than others."

Smiling, she nodded, but as she was going off, he called, "Put on your Levi's like the other morning. Leave your work clothes behind."

She nodded and disappeared up the stairs, skirting a corpse and an undertaker.

Rita had barely gone when Tulley burst in, scattergun

raised in a fist, attack-style, that and the badge on his shirt allowing him to bull right past Hub at the batwings.

For a moment, York thought the Rhomers had arrived after dark, after all.

But that wasn't it—Tulley had just heard about the excitement down to the Victory.

The eyes in the white-bearded face were wild. "I hate to 'bandon my post, Sheriff, but I thought mebbe you might need your ol' deputy."

York put a hand on the man's shoulder, while using his other hand to pull down the shotgun-waving arm.

"You did right, Tulley. I can use you right about now. And, anyway, smart money is on the Rhomers hitting town in sunlight."

He filled Tulley in on what had happened here. The undertaker was heading out, going after his wicker baskets, and the deputy took everything in with big eyes.

"Now," York said, "in just a short while, Miss Rita will be comin' down those steps with a travelin' bag in hand."

"She goin' somewheres?"

"She's going to a jail cell down at our office. You're going to accompany her there. And we'll leave your post at the stable untended for tonight. Just before sunup, you'll head over with your scattergun. Till then, Miss Rita is in your charge."

Tulley was frowning. "The gal *know* she's headin' for a jail cell?"

"Possibly not. Make her as comfortable as you can. Give her that large cell, way on the end. If she needs a meal, run down to the hotel restaurant and have them bring one up. And let her know all she has to do is call out and you'll walk her to the privy. Got all that?"

Tulley was shaking his head doubtfully. "This may not all be to her likin'."

"It may not. Be firm. You have a gun."

The deputy goggled at the sheriff. "Well, sir, ladies like Miss Rita, they has guns, too, sometimes."

"Little ones, Tulley. Not a great big one like you."

That made Tulley smile. He seemed mollified. And the thing was, York hoped Rita *would* have a gun amongst her things. If somebody got past him and Tulley, she might need to defend herself.

Because she was behaving very much like the kind of loose end this killer was tying off.

At the doors, York told Hub that if Rita wanted to re-open the Victory, that was fine—once the undertaker had hauled both corpses away.

"Might want to do some work with a mop first," York advised.

"Sheriff," Hub said dryly, "you have a good feel for business."

Out in front of the saloon, York emptied the two spent shells onto the boardwalk and reloaded with fresh bullets from his gun belt. He really didn't think the Rhomers would be dumb enough to attack at night. But the one Rhomer he'd had experience with turned out pretty damn dumb. So you never knew.

Right now he was on his way to talk to that bank president. It was time. The banker could wrap himself up in respectability all he wanted, but if he was also wrapping himself up in a duster and slashing the throats of young females, well, York would have to take exception.

Thomas Carter lived on the third floor of the brick bank building, above Doc Miller's surgery and sharing the same outdoor stairway, just up another landing. And Carter appeared to be home, several windows glowing with light. York climbed the two flights and knocked on the banker's door.

When he got no response, the sheriff knocked again, louder and more insistent; but still nothing.

He tried the door and found it unlocked. A lot of doors were left unlocked in a town this size, but for a man like Carter, that seemed surprising.

Entering a small kitchen, York announced himself, loudly, but again was not acknowledged. He moved into a living room arrayed with expensive-looking furniture in the Victorian style, button-back sofa, wingback chairs, marble-top tables, Oriental carpet. A bedroom with more heavy furnishings and striped wallpaper was uninhabited, as well, and so was a guest room.

"Mr. Carter! Sheriff York. Are you here?"

He was there, all right. In a study at a rolltop desk, where he was slumped, arms slack and hanging down, his head to one side, resting in a drying, darkening pool of blood. Carter was still attired in the same dark brown suit with embroidered vest he'd worn at the Citizens Committee meeting early this evening.

The side of the banker's head that was up had a small black hole in it, edged with red, dark red turned black. The one eye showing was blank, the mouth yawning open expressionlessly. The scorched smell of gunpowder was in the air.

Carter's right hand, at the end of a dangling arm, hung limp over a .45 Colt that rested on the floor, where he might have dropped it.

Might have dropped it, if this were a real suicide.

But York knew it wasn't.

Half an hour later, York was back at his office, where he dragged the chair from behind his desk back into the cell block. Tulley was seated outside the first cell, scattergun across his lap, his snoring no worse than a mountain rockslide.

York pulled the chair up and sat as Rita, seated on the edge of her cot, in a light blue shirt and Levi's and riding boots, glared at him.

"Lock me up," she said, "and put that old fool in charge of my safety? I can't even *sleep* with him sawing logs."

"You're not under arrest," he told her. "You can leave. But I believe, if you do, you stand to be killed."

"Locked in *here,* somebody could kill me."

Her traveling bag was on the floor next to her. He smiled. "Where is it?"

"Where's what?"

"Your derringer."

She huffed a laugh, smiled, and reached under the flat-looking pillow. She showed him the small, pearl-handled, silver gun.

"Your sister had one like that," he said.

She returned it to its hiding place. "This *is* my sister's. It was returned to me after she passed."

He had used that gun. He had killed Sheriff Harry Gauge with it. Thanks to Lola.

"We don't usually allow our prisoners," he said, "to hold on to their firearms."

"You said I wasn't a 'prisoner.' "

"Make that 'guest.' But you need to be on your own guard while you're here. I'm just one man."

Disgusted, she nodded toward the slumbering Tulley down the cell block. "And that desert rat isn't even *one* man."

"He might surprise you. Thomas Carter is dead, by the way."

"What?"

"Killed himself. At least that's what I'm supposed to think." He told her how he'd found the body, just a short while ago.

"Why *isn't* it a suicide?" she asked. "Maybe Carter killed that bank clerk and it wasn't so hard, but when he used a knife on poor Pearl, it made him realize what he'd done. What he'd become."

"Yeah, that's what somebody wants me to think."

"But you don't."

"No. And neither do you."

A dark eyebrow arched. "Don't I? What if I told you that Pearl shared with me what Upton told her—that Thomas Carter had embezzled funds and set up the robbery of his own bank to cover it up. What then?"

"Then I'd thank you for the information, and say you're right, but that only goes so far."

She got up and came over to the bars and stared through them at him, frowning. "It goes all the way, Caleb! You hounded that man into a terrible act with Pearl, and then into a state of mind where he took his own life."

York shook his head. "No, there's more to this than that. And I think you know what it is. Would you care to tell me?"

She folded her arms. "I don't have anything more to say."

He gestured with open palms. "Then you're not a guest. You *are* a prisoner."

She grabbed the bars and tried to shake them. "Damn you, Caleb York! Your killer *killed* himself! Can't you be satisfied with that?"

"I would have been," he said, standing, getting ready to haul his chair away from here, "if Doc Miller hadn't agreed with my diagnosis."

"What diagnosis?"

He sauntered off. "Good night, Rita. Sleep well. Let us know if you need the privy. Or you can make use of that chamber pot."

"*What diagnosis?*"

With a glance over his shoulder, he said, "That a man who shot himself in the head ought to have powder burns at the wound."

York left her stewing there.

In the meantime, he needed to catch some sleep, across the street in that pueblo, where a pallet awaited him. Morning would come soon enough, and with it the Rhomers.

CHAPTER FOURTEEN

Caleb York slept well, considering.

Not that the pending showdown would have hampered his ability to get some rest, but throughout the late evening, there had been the pounding of nails as boards were hammered over store windows, in anticipation of flying bullets.

This practice harked back to the days of Sheriff Harry Gauge's reign, when cowboys were allowed to tear up the town however they pleased, as long as they left their money at the Victory, which Gauge co-owned. The fearful preparation, all up and down Main Street, had lasted well past nine P.M.

After that, York slept, and slept soundly.

He'd had the pueblo hut to himself—three small rooms with a cooking area, some handmade furnishings, a couple of cots, and a trio of pallets, for the Gomez family who lived here. They had generously given their living quarters over to him, but even in the barrio, word of what was coming had got around. Where the Papa and Mama and three kiddies had spent the night was anybody's guess.

Outside the hole in the wall that was a window, Trinidad

had not yet woken up. York, who'd slept in his clothes with his holstered gun on a stubby chair nearby, stood and stretched and smoothed his black shirt and pants. He got into his boots and vest and slung on the .44 last, tying it down.

He usually woke around six and today seemed no exception. The eastern horizon would be blushing with rising sun soon if not already, and in half an hour, dawn would be here and, any time after that, so would the Rhomers.

The morning was cold, the wind stirring the dust in the barrio's single hard-mud street. York used the nearest outhouse, moving through wandering chickens to get to and from; a few dogs were stirring, too. Some cooking smells drifted, stovepipe chimneys promising coffee and chorizo and eggs; the "mamacitas" were up, but the "papacitos" likely still snoozed. Such a peaceful time of day in so peaceful a part of Trinidad.

Yet even here something was in the air besides cooking. Something tense. Eyes were on him. Women were murmuring. Even the animals sensed the stranger among them, and the danger he brought.

York crossed in the dark to the jailhouse, unlocked the front door and went inside. In the first cell, a slumbering Tulley was on the cot on his side, knees pulled up, looking like an ancient fetus. His snoring was gentle, compared to previously. The scattergun lay on the cell floor near him.

York picked the scattergun up, and Tulley didn't stir. It occurred to the sheriff that his deputy did not have the reflexes of a coiled cougar. He kicked the side of the cot, gently, shaking the chains that held it to the wall, and shaking Tulley, too. The old boy's eyes popped open and he jerked himself into a sitting position.

"Morning," York said.

Tulley snatched the scattergun from York's arms. "Is they here?"

"No. Sun won't be up for another fifteen, twenty minutes. Go heat up what's left of yesterday's coffee."

"It'll be strong enough to tear the bark offen a pine tree."

"Good."

Tulley nodded, tasted his mouth, and creaked to his feet. York let him by, then exited the cell and walked to the end of the cell block, where Rita in blouse and jeans was sitting on her cot, bare feet on the floor, rubbing a hand on her face.

"Sorry if we woke you," he said.

"If there's coffee," she said, "I'll take it."

"There will be, of a sort. And Tulley will walk you to the privy, if need be."

"Thanks."

A good distance separated them—him at the bars, her still seated on the cot against the far wall.

"Listen," he said, "you're gonna be alone here, real soon. I'm takin' a position elsewhere and so is my deputy. You keep that derringer handy."

She gestured vaguely. "Won't all the fun be going on out on the street?"

"I don't know where it'll be going on. But somebody might take advantage of the commotion to come in here and deal with you."

" 'Deal' with me how? *Deal* with me *why*?"

"Maybe you'd like to tell *me*, Rita. Then I could unlock that cell and you'd have more options."

She shook her head. "I have nothing more to say."

"Sorry to hear that."

Then she got quickly up and came over to the bars. She

gripped a bar with one hand, reached the other hand out to touch his face. He hadn't shaved.

"I do have something else to say," she said. "Try not to get yourself killed."

"See what I can do."

She shook her head. "You must be crazy, facing down five men."

He grinned at her. "Who said anything about facing them?"

She didn't know what to make of that.

Tulley brought her a tin cup of coffee. She tasted it, then gulped the sip, and said, "Well. That's an eye-opener."

"Thank ye, ma'am. But it was a mite better yesterday."

York took Tulley out into the office while their guest drank her coffee.

"You walk her to the privy," York said, "then take your post at the livery."

Tulley gave him a one-eye-open frown. "You seem shore they's comin' in that way."

"I'm not sure of anything, Tulley. But that's where the road from Las Vegas empties, and it'll put the sun at their backs."

Tulley made a twirly gesture with a forefinger. "They could fool ye and circle 'round and come in from the west end of Main."

"They could, but then I'd have the sun to *my* back. They may know enough to *not* want that."

"Iffen you say so."

"Tulley, the Rhomers don't know that I'm expectin' them. I figure them to come at me head on."

"If *I* was them," Tulley said, squinting shrewdly, "I'd spread my men around town, in the streets and alleys feedin' Main, a man or two in a winder prob'ly, and draw you out and cut you down."

"That's a good plan. But they aren't as smart as you, Tulley."

"They ain't?"

"No. They have guns but lack brains. Anyway, I'm counting on that. That and their desire for revenge."

"They's gettin' *paid,* remember."

"I haven't forgotten that. That's the one reason we could get surprised this morning—if they view me as a payday and not somebody they want to kill nice and slow."

York left Tulley to tend to their guest briefly before getting himself back to the livery, and his window onto Main.

As the sheriff walked toward the barrio, the lower third of the eastern sky glowed red-orange and bright yellow as if a distant fire was encroaching upon Trinidad.

In the barrio, the chickens and stray dogs still ruled, and the smoky cooking smells had heightened. That made his belly rumble, but he ignored its demands—you don't go into a gunfight on a full stomach. You might embarrass yourself puking at some point.

He positioned himself at the pueblo window.

Within minutes, the sun was spreading across the sky and illuminating a Main Street that might have belonged to a ghost town—not a soul in sight, no sign of waking businesses, only boarded-up windows and a street whose layer of river-sand was riffling in a too-cool breeze. No, not breeze.

Wind.

The kind that promises a storm.

And just about when he'd expected the Rhomers to ride in, black clouds rolled across the sky, churning, roiling, blotting out the sunrise, turning early morning into near midnight. Crackles of veiny lightning momentarily illuminated the sculpted, shifting forms of a burgeoning black thunderhead, billowing like smoke from some invisible conflagration.

Distant thunder shook the ceiling of the sky, and five men on horseback came riding in, harder than need be. They turned that corner past the livery, horses leaning; then their redheaded riders pulled back sharp on their reins and they assembled in front of the jail, one man on horseback moving out in front of the others.

These horses, York was pleased to see, were not the black mustangs he feared might show up under the Rhomer backsides—that type of well-trained steed of which three dead bank robbers had availed themselves. These were solid horses, all right, but as mixed a bunch as the redheaded brothers were similar. Two quarter horses, two paints, an Appaloosa.

It took the horses a while to settle, and the men on them seemed worked up, too. Grinning yellow teeth in scruffy red-bearded faces, butts moving up and down on saddles.

They weren't interchangeable, though, these Rhomers. The one out front—positioning himself as the leader, as the men on horseback faced the adobe jailhouse—was older, and looked a lot like the late Vint Rhomer.

He'd likely be Lem.

One brother was skinny and tall, another was heavy and short, the other two medium-size, but of those two, one was obviously the youngest, just a kid in his early twenties, his beard barely filled in. All were dressed in Levi's and shirts with sleeve garters and vests, of various colors—maybe this family shopped together. Only a variety of hats set them apart.

One thing they had in common: .45 Colts in tied-down holsters, kept in place by snap straps. They must have bought their guns together, too. They had rifles in scabbards, as well, riding with them.

The horses were settled. Each brother unsnapped his holster.

Quietly, Lem—York barely made it out, listening at his pueblo window—said to his brothers, "Second he shows, let rip."

The sky grumbled and the horses shuffled a little.

When the animals had settled again, Lem called out, "*Caleb York! Lem Rhomer. You killed my brother Vint. I mean to see you die for it.*"

York wondered how many nights under the stars Lem Rhomer had spent, staring into the sky, composing those words.

Lem wasn't through: "*Come out and face me like a man, and we'll have it out. My brothers been told, if the fight is fair, they is to ride off. Caleb York! You hear me?*"

The sky alone answered with a faint, murmuring rumble. The horses danced a little. Settled again.

"*York, come out here and meet me in the street. They say you're fast! Well so am I. Let's see who's the better man!*"

Tulley burst out the barnlike doors of the livery and fired both barrels of the scattergun into the sky. The thunder of it, here on the ground before God could have his say, spooked the horses bad. Every one of the animals got up on its hind legs and shrieked in terror and then bucked and circled and danced and kicked, and one by one, each redheaded Rhomer got tossed from his saddle onto the sandy street.

York came out of the pueblo hut as the two closest to him were trying to scramble to their feet, guns in hand but wholly flummoxed.

Somebody yelled, "*He's over there!*"

The two—the medium-sized pair, one of whom was the youngest brother—wheeled toward York, but their guns weren't even raised when a bullet blew through the eye of the older of the pair, and a second slug cracked the younger one's head like an eggshell. They stood momentarily, staring with three blank eyes, then flopped back onto the street and leaked blood and brains.

Tulley scurried back inside the livery, while the other three Rhomers, Lem included, realized they'd been ambushed, and been abandoned by their spooked horses, who had gone off this way and that, and the remaining three brothers ran down deserted Main Street, looking for cover.

Like a delayed echo of Tulley's scattergun blasts, the sky ruptured with thunder and rain sheeted down. York ran to the boardwalk opposite the jail and, with his back to the building facades, moved down slow. The rain came almost straight down, making a translucent curtain. York barely made out the heavyset Rhomer cut around the corner of First Street, down to the right, and the skinny one do the same, on the other side of the street.

Lem Rhomer, who York guessed was the most dangerous of this bunch, he'd lost track of. That probably meant the man had ducked into one of the few buildings whose doors weren't locked—that would be the hotel or the Victory and maybe the café.

First things first.

The rain drummed incessantly on the roof over the boardwalk as York moved cautiously down. Whip cracks of lightning momentarily lit up the night this morning had become, but no Rhomers were in sight. Skinny was around one corner, Fatty the other, the one York was inching toward. At some point he might become a good target for the former, although either man, or both, might not be waiting—they may have splashed through back alleys to either flee or find a better position.

At least he knew neither man was tucked into a recession of the buildings he was edging past—although, come to think of it, *Lem* could be. At each one, York peeked around, ready to blast, finding nothing but closed doors. As the angry sky roared and the rain pelted the boardwalk awning, he slid along and, finally, made it to the corner.

Peeking around, he saw nothing but a street between buildings that was turning into a soup of sand and mud, as Main Street's businesses trailed off into residences.

He stepped off the boardwalk onto ground already gone spongy and the rain pummeled and drenched him, gathering in his curl-brimmed hat and overflowing, as he moved toward the rear alley. Again, recessions of doorways presented danger, and he took care with the two doors between him and the alley.

When at last he rounded the corner into the alley—which bordered fenced-off residence yards at left—he saw nothing, though at right a rear exterior stairway to living quarters above a store had a landing that presented a platform for a shooter. But in the dense downpour, York couldn't see anybody up there.

He decided to go up and make sure.

With the .44 in his right hand, York couldn't make use of the wooden railing, so his left hand supported him against the side of the clapboard building. The rain was pounding into his face, but his hat brim was protecting his eyes somewhat, as he went up one step—one slow step—at a time.

He was halfway up when a roar came not from the sky but from a small bear of a man, a redheaded bearded bear, who had been prone on that landing and now lumbered to his feet and pointed down with his .45, though the dripping monstrosity was just a blur before York's rain-streaked eyes.

York's two .44 slugs made their own thunder, punching the fat Rhomer in the chest, shaking him, rocking him, making him stumble backward and he went over the far side of the landing, taking some crunching wood with him. He must already have been dead, because he didn't scream on the trip down, though when he landed on the muddy-topped ground, he hit hard enough to send plenty of moisture momentarily back into the sky, the *whump* of it competing with a halfhearted growl of thunder.

York went down the steps much quicker than he'd come up, and he slogged toward the street, knowing he had to risk crossing Main to seek the skinny brother. He would stay low and he would move as quickly as this molasses underfoot would allow. But he had barely begun the journey when he realized someone was running at him, shooting.

The skinny Rhomer!

.45 slugs flying overhead, York flopped to the ground and was aiming up at the screaming, approaching scarecrow when a boom came that wasn't from the sky. The skinny guy suddenly was a teetering headless thing with a jagged neck geysering red and getting it spewed right back.

Grinning, a thoroughly sopped Tulley came into view, his scattergun barrels smoking despite the rain.

The skinny brother wobbled, then fell headfirst onto the ground. Well, not *exactly* headfirst. . . .

Tulley scurried over and helped York up.

"*That* stopped him," Tulley said.

"Seemed to," York said.

Pieces of what had once ridden the skinny one's shoulders were scattered in the rain-swept street, looking like nothing remotely human, except for a staring eyeball, floating in a puddle.

"That leaves one," Tulley said, over the downpour. "That Lem feller."

"See where he went?"

The deputy pointed. "Down the block from the Victory. Think he ducked in that there doorway. Barbershop."

They moved to the edge of the building. Behind them was the dead fat Rhomer, on his back, his mouth open and overflowing with rain. In front of them, in the street, the headless skinny Rhomer lay on his belly.

As if a switch had been thrown, the rain slowed and then stopped. Dark clouds still filled the sky, but they were moving fast, racing, a stampede headed elsewhere.

Within a minute, the only raindrops were those falling from awnings, and the sky turned a tentative blue, damn near cloudless. The soggy aftermath was everywhere, pooled in the street, dripping off storefronts.

But the storm had passed. The one in the sky, at least.

York quickly crossed the side street to take a position alongside the opposite building, the mercantile. Tulley came along, and fell in, in back of him. The old boy was reloading. So was York.

"*Lem Rhomer!*" the sheriff called around the corner. "*Give yourself up! Your brothers are dead. You don't have to be!*"

The street was silent but for *drip-drip-drips.*

Then: "*Why not decide this, York!*"

Yes—the recession of the barbershop doorway. Just across the way and down. Well within range. . . .

"*What is there to decide, Rhomer?*"

More silence punctuated by the aftermath of the deluge.

Then: *"What do you think, you bastard? Who's fastest!"*

"That's what you want, Rhomer?"

"That's what I want! Face-to-face. I'm holstering my gun, right now. You holster yours."

"And if I do?"

"I step out and we finish this! See just how fast Caleb York really is!"

"All right!"

Several long seconds dragged by.

Rhomer stepped out.

York stepped out.

Turned sideways, presenting smaller targets, they faced each other in, and across, the saturated street.

But Rhomer's holster was empty, his gun already drawn and at his side, held rib-cage-high, the turn of his body meant to conceal the trick.

Then one last thunder crack came: a .44 slug from York's gun—he'd done the same as Rhomer, been ready with holster empty and gun in hand and rib-cage-high.

The bullet punched the last redheaded brother in the belly, .45 tumbling out of his fingers, Lem Rhomer himself tumbling into the street, facedown, exposing the cavernous red-bubbling exit wound the .44 round left behind.

As York hurried to the man, Tulley tagging after, Rhomer crawled over onto his back, filling his red-bearded face with morning sun, though his clothes were filthy from the muddy street, the brown covering him leavened only by the scarlet, spreading patch over his belly where the bullet had gone in.

Rhomer looked up at York; gut-shot like that, the man was suffering, the pain excruciating. But he still said, "Damn . . . damn liar. . . ."

"You know the saying," York said blandly, looking down at the dying man. " 'Takes one to know one.' "

Tulley was at York's side. "Put him out of his misery, Sheriff. It'll take him a long damn time to die iffen you don't. . . . He be way past doctorin'."

"No."

Tulley took York's sleeve. Whispering, the coot said, "*Do* it, Caleb. You'd shoot a dog in the head, sufferin' like that."

The sheriff responded to his deputy, but he was staring at the grimacing Rhomer, who glared back in pain and rage.

York said, "Dogs don't need to think about what they done."

Tulley scuttled off. Couldn't stand the sight.

But Caleb York stayed and watched the man die.

CHAPTER FIFTEEN

The sun was out and so were the citizens of Trinidad. They hugged the rails of the boardwalks, men and women, some of them fathers and mothers with their children along for the view of the aftermath of a shootout that for all its gory glory would grow into epic proportions as the story was passed from this one to that, as eyewitnesses (who had seen nothing, cowering under tables or hugging floors) described in vivid detail the day Sheriff Caleb York gunned down the five Rhomer brothers.

Or was that seven Rhomer brothers? Or had there been a dozen of the redheaded villains who had gone down under the relentless fire of Caleb York's blazing six-shooters (like the brothers, the number of York's guns would increase over the years).

Today, however, eyes were wide and at a distance as the doctor and undertaker approached the sheriff, who was standing over the body of Lem Rhomer, a big ugly man, who had died wearing a big ugly grimace. The sand on the street had returned to its damp riverbank roots, a wealth of puddles and pools resisting the sun's rays.

But there was no question: the sky was bright and blue and the violence was over.

As they regarded a corpse that still seemed in pain, Caleb York said to Doc Miller, "You have four more dead patients scattered here and there. My deputy will show you to them."

"Perkins has already spotted one of 'em," Doc Miller said, nodding toward where the dour-faced undertaker, as always in black frock coat and beaver high hat, looked down regretfully at a headless skinny Rhomer brother sprawled in the moist sand.

"Looks disappointed," York said, "for a man about to make ten dollars."

The doc smirked. "It's a bitter pill, knowing he dasn't display a corpse like that in his window." Miller gave York a look. "You know, I haven't had a *live* patient in two days. If I have to write out one more death certificate, I'll be riding over to Ellis and have that print shop make me some forms."

"Well," York said, with a sigh and a glance around, "things should be quieter now. Can you and Perkins handle these dead ones?" He gestured to his soaked, mud-splotched attire. "I need to clean up some."

"Before cleaning up the town?"

"I do have more to do on that score," York admitted.

The doctor said he'd take charge of the various deceased, and the sheriff called his deputy over to have him give Miller and Perkins a tour of the carnage.

York was on his way to the hotel, where he could get a bath—the place had plumbing from its well, though it would cost fifty cents to get the tub of water heated up by firewood—when the telegraph operator came rushing up to him, already heated up. The scrawny, bespectacled Parsons—like the rest of the citizens of Trinidad—was dry and clean. But he was also excited.

The little man handed York a wire, saying, "This just came in for you, Sheriff. All the way from New York City."

"Thanks, Ralph." He dug a dime out of his soggy pocket and tossed the slippery coin to the operator.

A clearly troubled Parsons lingered, however, saying, "That's *dynamite*, Sheriff."

York was reading it. "I agree, Ralph. But can I count on you to keep it to yourself this time? My dime cover that?"

The operator flushed, nodded, and scurried off.

Right outside the hotel, York paused when a voice called out to him, *"Sheriff!"*

He turned and a smiling Zachary Gauge was approaching quickly, again in his frock coat, waistcoat, and silk tie, looking like a parson with a wealthy flock.

York smiled slightly as he accepted and shook the offered hand. "What brings you to town, Zachary? Did you want a ringside seat on the festivities?"

"I stayed the night here at the hotel," he said, with a nod toward the place. "But it had nothing to do with those outlaws coming to town—I have a business meeting with our town shopkeepers. On my way now."

"Over at the mercantile?"

"That's right. I just wanted to tell you how pleased I am that things worked out the way they did. You're a real force of nature, Sheriff."

"That storm wasn't *my* work."

Half a grin blossomed. "But I have a feeling you made it work for you. One man against five. Amazing."

"There were two of us. Deputy Tulley pitched in."

"I haven't heard the details. Just that you prevailed, handily. At any rate, I must be off."

York gestured to his mud-spattered self. "I'm going in and get a mite more presentable. Would you stop over at the sheriff's office, after your meeting? In a hour and a half, say?"

Zachary's eyebrows rose. "Certainly. Anything special you wish to discuss?"

"A couple things I'd like to go over."

And went down. "Certainly. An hour and a half should be fine."

Zachary tipped his black flat-brimmed Stetson and made briskly for Harris Mercantile.

York went into the hotel lobby and over to the check-in desk to arrange for his hot bath.

In clean clothes, shaved, and fully washed—though he'd had a bath just three days before—York felt almost human again. As he got dressed in his hotel room, he realized he was getting into the dudish apparel—his usual black, but with gray trim on cuffs and pearl buttons down the front—that had caused some to underestimate him when he first rode into town, a stranger.

He cleaned off his curl-brimmed hat as best he could, though it might be time for a new one, and cleaned the mud from his hand-tooled boots, the only pair he owned. The .44 would need cleaning and oiling, but for now he just wiped it off with the towel with which he'd dried himself, and used a slightly damp cloth to clean the mud from his gun belt, knowing it deserved (and would receive) better.

By the time he was heading up the boardwalk to the jailhouse, trading nods and smiles with townsfolk (ladies giggling, men tipping hats), York found Main Street looking close to dry and wholly absent of dead Rhomers or parts thereof. The doctor and undertaker, and for that matter his deputy, had done their part.

Zachary Gauge wouldn't likely show up for another fifteen minutes yet, which was fine because York had a few things he wanted to do first. He tossed the telegram, facedown, on his desk, grabbed the big key ring off the wall, and strolled through the doorless doorway into the cell block.

In the first cell, Tulley was sleeping again, on his back on the cot, for once not snoring. Momentarily, York suspected his deputy had celebrated with a bottle, but it appeared the man was just plumb exhausted. The old boy had had a busy morning, at that.

York found Rita pacing in her oversized cell. Earlier, she'd been barefoot, but now she was in her own hand-tooled boots, her dark hair down and brushing her shoulders. Without the face paint, she looked young. She also looked impatient.

"Congratulations on not being dead," she said, pausing in her pacing, not looking happy about it at all. "Killed five more men, did you? How many is that?"

"Haven't done the ciphering yet. I'll get back to you."

"Very funny. How about letting me out now?"

"Actually, I *am* letting you out."

"About time!"

"And moving you down to a different cell."

"*What?*"

"I want you closer to the office, but not in that first cell, where you can be seen from out there."

She was frowning at him. "Are you serious, Sheriff?"

"Dead serious about keeping you alive."

He unlocked the cell.

"Bring your bag," he said.

She huffed an exasperated sigh, but complied. When he'd locked her into cell number two, she asked, "What is this about?"

"There's a conversation I want you to hear. You just keep mum, all right? I'll bring you into it if I feel it's necessary."

She was frowning again. "Conversation with whom?"

He grinned at her. "That would ruin it."

Then he went into cell number one and kicked Tulley's cot, hard. The former desert rat reacted as if woken by an earthquake.

"Up and at 'em, boy," York said.

Tulley blinked his eyes into focus. "What's left to do today?"

"I have a guest coming. I want you on the porch with that loaded scattergun handy."

"In case your guest gets inhospitable?"

"No, in case you spot a rabbit or a squirrel."

The deputy's eyes narrowed. "You're joshin', right? That's you bein' *dry*, ain't it, Sheriff?"

"After that storm, it's nice bein' dry, don't you think?" He pointed in the direction of the porch. "Just sit out there and don't let anybody or anything interrupt me. If you hear something happen in the office—"

"Like what?"

"You'll know. It's guard duty, Tulley. Beats night patrol, don't you think?"

"Shore does."

So Tulley got positioned on the porch with the scattergun across his lap, and York stood out there with him, looking at sunshine improving the day, hands on hips, waiting for his guest.

Five minutes or so later, Zachary stepped up onto the porch and gave Tulley a nod and York a smile and a nod. "Apologies if I'm late."

York waved it off. "I don't have a timepiece, anyway. Tell me you're early and I'll believe you."

The two men went into the office, the sheriff closing the door.

York got behind his desk and sat in his chair, getting comfortable, leaning back, his right ankle resting on his knee, his hands folded on his flat belly, his hat back on his head. Zachary, his frock coat unbuttoned, took off his Stetson and rested it on the edge of the desk, to his right. Nothing was on the scarred wooden surface between them but the facedown wire.

York said, "I hope your business meeting went well."

Zachary's smile under the thin mustache was equally thin, but wide. "It did indeed. You may be aware that my late cousin pulled a fast one on these shopkeepers, investing in their establishments and then demanding repayment for that investment while holding on to a fifty percent interest. Such a shameless exercise in human greed."

"That's just about the only kind."

"Pardon?"

"Of greed. The human kind. Never knew an animal that was greedy, except maybe for food. But that's 'cause they never know where or when their next meal is comin' from."

Zachary shrugged. "Perhaps that's the human motivation as well." He shifted in the chair. "Getting back to my cousin's skullduggery ... when I heard that these local men of business had sought legal help in Albuquerque, to resolve this matter, I felt I ought to nip it in the bud."

"How so?"

His smile was edged with pride. "I've signed their shops back to them in exchange for a modest ten percent interest."

"Well, you must be popular in town about now."

Zachary shrugged. "I just want to be a constructive

member of this community. We're also talking about the reorganization of the bank, now that Mr. Carter's suicide has left that institution in disarray. Apparently he left no surviving relations."

York gave him a wry grin. "Not even a cousin?"

That got a small laugh out of Zachary. "Not even a cousin. Uh, Sheriff, let me say, again, how impressed I am by how you've handled yourself in this difficult situation. I've heard in some detail, now, exactly how you handled those brutes this morning. A remarkable performance."

Still leaning back, ankle on knee, arms folded, York smiled and said, "I appreciate that, comin' from you. After all, you've given a pretty damn remarkable performance yourself."

Zachary's forehead frowned, though his mouth smiled. "How is that . . . ?"

The sheriff shrugged easily. "Everything that's happened over these past days is the work of your skilled hand, starting with robbing the bank."

Zachary took that like a slap, blinked, shook his head as if his hearing might be bad, opened his mouth wide, then finally laughed.

"The *bank*? Sheriff, are you sure you didn't take a blow to the head in that fracas this morning? What would *I* know about robbing banks? I wasn't even in *town* when First Bank was robbed!"

"Not in town, but in the area. Certainly as close as Las Vegas, anyway, and possibly your ranch. You had deals worked out, in advance, with certain individuals—your foreman, Gil Willart, for example. And with Rita Filley, regarding the Victory, of which you didn't even ask her for ten percent, like you just did the shopkeepers."

Zachary seemed genuinely amused. "Go on, Sheriff.

This is a fascinating story. You might be able to interest that Buntline character in it, for one of his dime novels."

"It does have that flavor, I grant you. You see, Gil Willart was a regular of that prostitute Pearl, at the Victory. Willart learned from her what her bank-clerk beau told her—that Herbert Upton would be soon getting a promotion and a raise, and maybe even a substantial sum beyond that. Because Upton knew Thomas Carter was embezzling."

He shrugged a little. "Interesting theory."

"I figure you met with the bank president in Las Vegas, or possibly out at the Circle G. You spun a plan to help the banker cover up his financial shortfall and at the same time feather your nest. You arranged for some of your cousin Harry's bunch to rob that bank, and the money was turned back over to you."

Zachary's eyes went wide. "To *me?*"

"To you. So you could ride in on a white horse, or anyway an Appaloosa, with enough money to shore up the bank in its difficulties. Money you brought from back East, where you liquidated your substantial assets. Only there *were* no substantial assets back East. What you had to deposit in the bank, with Carter's full knowledge and collusion, was the money that had been *stolen* from it."

For several endless seconds, the two men just looked coldly at each other.

Finally, Zachary said, "And why the hell would I do that?"

"To become a constructive member of the community, and to draw on that stolen money to buy stock for your land-rich, cattle-poor ranch."

Zachary chuckled as he shook his head. "You have much more imagination, Sheriff, than I would ever have dreamed. What next? Am I a murderer, too? Did I kill that fool of a clerk Upton? And, what—banker Carter, too?"

"Carter killed his own grasping clerk. That little worm was just one accomplice too many in this thing. I doubt you gave your blessing, though, because it only complicated matters. Probably led you to feel that our distinguished bank president was coming apart at the seams. And he—and probably you, too, Zachary—sensed I was onto him. *That's* why you killed him and staged that suicide."

His broad smile said how ridiculous that sounded. "What was staged about it?"

"All of it. You shot him from across the room, or at least at enough distance not to leave powder burns at the wound. For all your careful planning, and it was shrewd and clever, I admit . . . things were starting to unravel. With Upton dead, the grieving, laudanum-addled Pearl became a particularly dangerous loose end. So you used your knife—where did an Easterner come up with a Smoky Mountain toothpick like that?—and you snipped her off good. Sneaked up the back stairs from the alley, wearing that duster in anticipation of a blood shower. You *have* been around, Zachary. You have been around."

"Have I."

"You have. Now, let's talk about the Rhomers. You sent your man Gil Willart to Las Vegas to hire the brothers to come shoot me down—looking to get revenge, everybody would think. The really cunning touch was telling me yesterday that *you* suspected Gil had done as much. Then I killed him for you, though in my defense he did draw down on me. But still—that's a loose end I snipped for you. And you haven't even thanked me."

This time the smile had a sneer in it. "I do thank you,

Sheriff, for sharing this entertaining flight of fancy. And it's nothing more than that, because you haven't a shred of proof to back it up."

"I have this," York said, and he flipped over the wire. "Read it yourself. Or I can sum it up. My friends at Pinkerton's recognized your name right away. Your only connection to Wall Street is as a swindler. Several rich women have died while they knew you. You've been tried half-a-dozen times, though never convicted. You are known to have left New York and its environs over a month ago. I'm gonna say you came West, young man."

"Droll. Very droll."

"Zachary Gauge is a notorious bunco artist, not a legitimate businessman who liquidated his funds. You've never been married and suffered the various tragedies that people around town are discussing so sympathetically. I imagine you shared that melodrama with Willa Cullen, too. She's a smart girl but no match for the likes of a sharper like you."

Zachary, who had only glanced at the telegram, picked it up and tossed it toward York, with casual indifference. "So what? Everybody who comes West is escaping something. We're all starting over."

"You decided to start over when you received this windfall, thanks to your cousin's death, inheriting all this land in the heart of cattle country. You probably didn't realize till you got here—a month earlier than is generally known—that while you did have plenty of land, you also had no beef. So you fell back into your scheming ways."

Zachary gave him the kind of look reserved for a madman. "Scheming ways like giving the shopkeepers here their businesses back? Asking only a nominal ten percent?"

"Well, that was a problem you solved smoothly. You

had a lot of names back East, but your *real* one, with all its nasty baggage, is Zachary Gauge. And to collect your inheritance, you had to stick with it. If that lawyer in Albuquerque went digging, he'd have found out who Zachary Gauge really is—a confidence man and suspected murderer."

No smile now. "You still don't have a damned thing, York."

"We have a bloodstained duster that you bought some-where around here, possibly right at Harris Mercantile."

Zachary batted that away. "How many dusters like that have been sold in this town in the last six months? Anyway, there's nothing to tie me to that whore's killing."

Still leaning back lazily, York said, "Well, I have a strong witness who can likely link you to that murder, and a lot else. Rita saw you exit Pearl's crib all covered in blood and make your exit out the back stairs of the Victory. She was on your side before things started getting nasty. But one of her girls getting her throat cut like that . . . that can weigh heavily on a good woman."

"There's nothing good about that dance-hall whore," Zachary said bitterly. Then he grinned nastily. "But you still don't have a witness—Rita skipped town last night. Packed her bag and ran out of the Victory and went off who-knows-where."

"Oh, I know where." York unfolded his arms to gesture toward the cell block. "She's well within earshot. That's right, she's heard everything we've been saying. No, I'll have plenty about you to share with the circuit judge when he comes through."

Zachary scowled and straightened his tie, and then his hand went swiftly under his coat and came back with a small pocket revolver that was swinging York's way when the sheriff whipped the Smoky Mountain toothpick from the boot resting on his ankle and flung the knife with force across the desk and into Zachary's chest, where it entered with a resounding *thunk*.

The revolver clunked to the floor.

The razor-sharp blade was deep in the man's heart, but Zachary wasn't quite dead yet. York had just time enough.

"Thought you'd like your knife back," he said.

CHAPTER SIXTEEN

When Zachary Gauge went backward, taking his chair with him and breaking it into kindling, the noise was enough to summon Tulley from his perch on the porch.

The deputy and his scattergun came bursting in, like the fort was being attacked. He came to a sudden stop when he saw the blank-eyed Zachary Gauge staring up at a heaven surely denied him.

"Well, sir," Tulley said, eyes wide, scratching the side of his head with his free hand, "that there's one way to bust up an engagement."

"Round up Miller and Perkins," Caleb York said, "and get back here."

"Them two's shore doin' land-office business," Tulley said as he went out, shaking his shaggy head.

With just the barest glance at the dead swindler, York came out from around his desk and walked back into the cell block.

Rita was sitting on her cot, eyes wide, a hand over her mouth.

"You heard?" he asked.

She swallowed, nodded. "You . . . killed him? With . . . the knife he used . . . on Pearl . . . ?"

York nodded. "It was a boot knife, and that's where I had it. I thought he might try something, so I kept it near at hand."

She didn't come to him, just stayed right there on the cot, its wall-chains whining some. "How did you know I'd seen him leaving all bloody?"

"I didn't."

Her eyes were wide and pleading. "Caleb, the only thing I knew was that Zachary was in the area weeks ahead of when he pretended to get here. That's how he made his deal with me. Not through the mails."

"I never exactly believed that."

"You didn't challenge me."

"Why call you a liar and get on your bad side? You make a better friend than enemy."

She blinked at him. "Were you . . . using me?"

"Why, you never used anybody?"

Her eyes stared into nothing. "He . . . he would have killed *me* next."

"That's right. Right there in that cell, unless you got him with your derringer first."

She swallowed; she looked very small. "What happens now?"

York shrugged. "Things take their due course, startin', I'd imagine, with whatever's in Zachary's account at the bank being returned to the depositors. If the papers have been signed, the Cullens should wind up with the Gauge land . . . an unexpected result of his swindle."

"He'd have killed Willa, too."

York shrugged. "When he got around to it, maybe. Or maybe he hoped to change his ways, when things settled down. People do come West for a new life."

Rita seemed to be studying him. "And people leave

towns like Trinidad for a new life, too. Is that what you'll do?"

"Not right away. I'm stayin' awhile. I helped make this mess. Least I can do is help clean it up."

"What about Willa? What about that girl of yours?"

His answer was a shrug. Then: "I'll have Tulley let you out. Gather your things."

She started doing that and York went out into the office where Tulley was coming in with the doc trailing behind him.

"Undertaker'll be here shortly," Tulley said. "Really keepin' him hoppin' today."

Miller was looking down at the dead, staring Zachary, on his back on the busted chair. "This one'll perk Perkins up. Just right for his window."

"I'll leave you to it," York said, in no mood for banter. He felt all talked out, though there was still talking left to do and no way to avoid it.

Walking over to the livery, where his gelding waited in its stall, York knew that he had not yet faced the day's biggest challenge.

He still had a difficult call to make out to the Cullen place.

About the Authors

MICKEY SPILLANE and MAX ALLAN COLLINS collaborated on numerous projects, including twelve anthologies, three films, and the *Mike Danger* comic-book series.

Spillane was the best-selling American mystery writer of the twentieth century. He introduced Mike Hammer in *I, the Jury* (1947), which sold in the millions, as did the six tough mysteries that soon followed. The controversial P.I. has been the subject of a radio show, comic strip, and several television series, starring Darren McGavin in the 1950s and Stacy Keach in the '80s and '90s. Numerous gritty movies have been made from Spillane novels, notably director Robert Aldrich's seminal film *noir, Kiss Me Deadly* (1955), and *The Girl Hunters* (1963), in which the writer played his own famous hero.

Collins has earned an unprecedented twenty-two Private Eye Writers of America "Shamus" nominations, winning for the novels *True Detective* (1983) and *Stolen Away* (1993) in his Nathan Heller series, and for "So Long, Chief," a Mike Hammer short story begun by Spillane and completed by Collins. His graphic novel *Road to Perdition* is the basis of the Academy Award–winning film. A filmmaker in the Midwest, he has had half-a-dozen feature screenplays produced, including *The Last Lullaby* (2008), based on his innovative Quarry novels, also the basis of a current Cinemax TV series. As "Barbara Allan," he and his wife, Barbara, write the "Trash 'n' Treasures" mystery series (recently *Antiques Swap*).

Both Spillane (who died in 2006) and Collins received the Private Eye Writers life achievement award, the Eye.